Holding Back The Years

Holding Back The Years

Kasha Thompson

WEBSTER AVENUE PUBLISHING
LINCOLN, CA

HOLDING BACK THE YEARS

Paperback ISBN: 979-8-9862679-1-3

Copyright © 2022 by Kasha Thompson

All rights reserved. No part of this book may be reproduced in any form or by any electronic or mechanical means, including information storage and retrieval systems, without written permission from the author, except for the use of brief quotations in a book review.

This book is a work of fiction. Names, characters, places, and incidents are the product of the author's imagination or are used fictitiously. Any resemblance to actual events, locales, or persons, living or dead, is strictly coincidental.

This edition published and arranged by Webster Avenue Publishing.

Printed in the United States of America. First Edition October, 2022

Character Illustration by: Beka Giorgadze

Cover Design by: Webster Avenue Publishing

Editing: Courtney Driver of Whoproofedit.com

content note

Please note Holding Back the Years discusses topics which could potentially trigger certain audiences. Some readers may consider the following as spoilers.

- Coarse Language: Moderate
- Sex: Several sexually explicit scenes
- Elder Care & Senior Care Facilities
- Alzheimer's Disease
- Marital infidelity of supporting characters

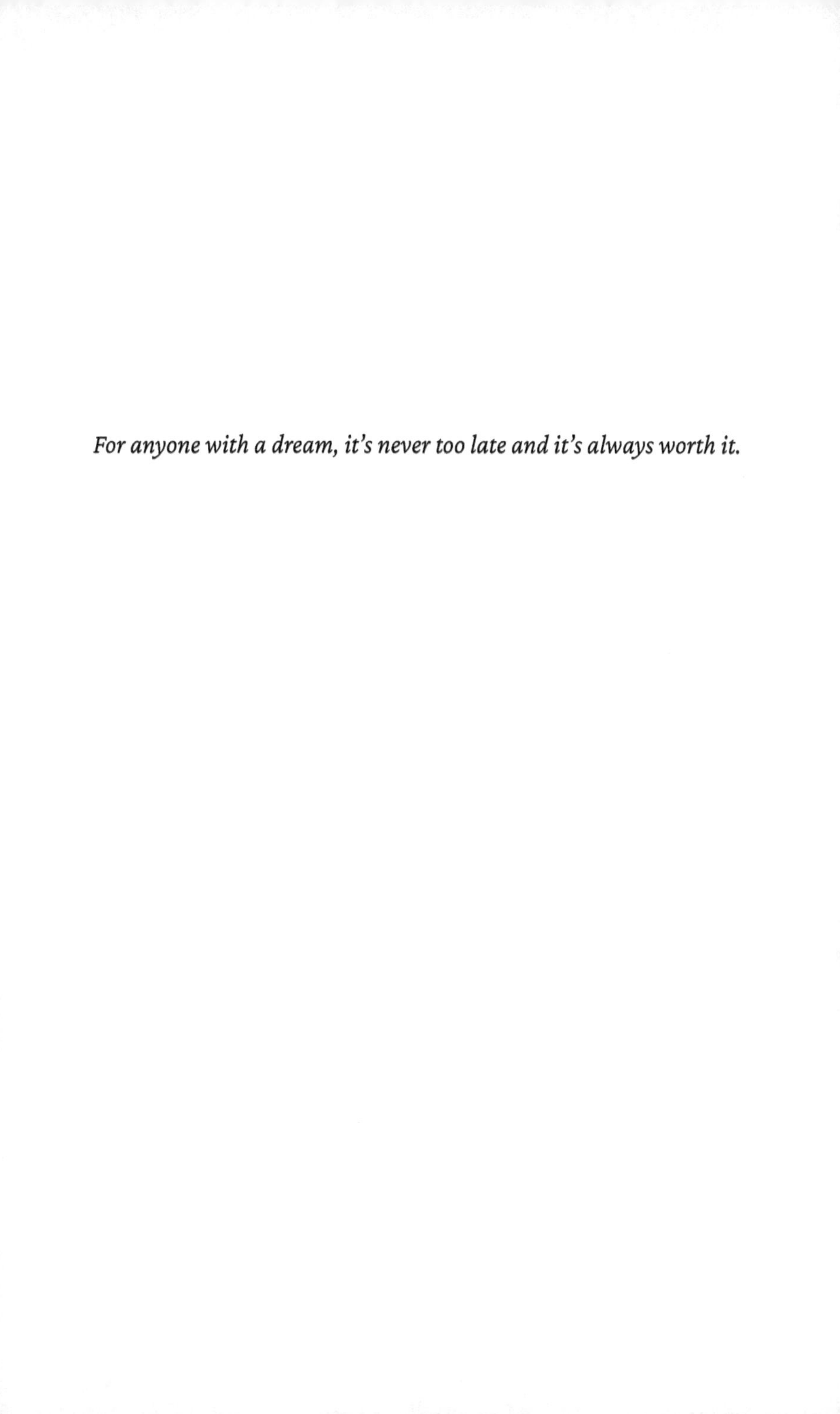

For anyone with a dream, it's never too late and it's always worth it.

<h1 style="text-align:center">one</h1>

SERAPHINA

"IS IT ON?" Pops asked.

"It's recording now." I reassured my grandfather.

"Testing, testing," he said, projecting his voice into my cell phone.

"Pops, you can just talk normally. No need to yell." I tried not to laugh as he fidgeted with his plaid shirt as if more than his voice was being recorded.

"So where do you want me to start?" he asked.

"The beginning is as good a place as any." With a click of my pen, I sat ready to take notes on his musings.

"Well, I reckon my first memory was my daddy in his faded denim shirt and jeans heading off to work every morning. He had a yellow lunch pail." Pops chuckled with a shake of his head. "My daddy hated that yellow pail but it was all they had left at the store so my momma picked it up."

I listened intently as Pops reminisced about his youth. It took months, and all the persuasion skills I'd learned in journalism school, for him to agree to finally sit down and open up. For thirty-three years Pops had been my favorite teacher. He taught me how to reel in my first fish. He taught me how to position the rifle in between my shoulder blades making sure it was steady before taking a shot. He shared a ton of useful life hacks, but for all that teaching he never did a lot of talking. Not about the things that really mattered at least.

"So, your great-uncle Billy and I went running off down that street with Mr. Sims hot on our heels. For an old man he was faster than he ought to be," Pops said while slapping his knee and coughing out a laugh.

I laughed too, imagining Pops, an eight-year-old boy who from his retelling was a bit of a trouble maker.

Pops's smile faded and a puzzled expression crossed his face. "Seraphina, is this the kinda stuff you were looking for?"

"Yes, this stuff is great. I want to know everything about you."

"I promise you my life wasn't that interesting." He raised a bewildered shoulder.

"You mean isn't that interesting. You're still currently in the midst of living that life."

"If you can call this living," Pops said, waving his hand around the room.

"I thought you were starting to like this place? That you'd made some friends."

Pops sucked his teeth. "The last thing I needed was new friends. What I need is to be back in my own home."

Reaching for his hand, I tried to keep my tone soft and calm like the nurses had instructed. "I know that's what you want and Dad tried to make it work—"

"Lie, that's a lie. He didn't try, he gave in." Pops worked his mouth into a crooked frown.

This was always a sore subject, one I didn't want to linger on. "Do you know why I kept bugging you to sit down with me to discuss your life?"

"Because you're nosy. Always have been since you were a little girl." Pops replied with a straight face.

"OK, rude." I shrugged his words off. "I wanted to talk because your life is interesting because you lived it. And that life produced my dad who eventually had me. That's quite the legacy to be the grandfather of Seraphina Jacobs." I teased.

"Don't know what's so interesting about a man working all his life to support his family."

He disagreed with me which he often did. That was one of the things I liked most about Pops; he was always going to tell me what he thought even if it was in stark contradiction to my own beliefs. His opinions made for some good conversations. My father never understood why I entertained Pops's antiquated thinking. But his beliefs, no matter how outdated some of them remained, were based on years of experience I didn't have. So, I decided to take the good and ignore the bad.

"I just realized your life was so much more than being my granddaddy. I want to memorialize that life so my future children and your grandkids and great-grands know who you are and what you mean to this family."

"OK, you already convinced me once I don't need to be convinced a second time."

There was a light knock at the door followed by Nurse Irma entering the room. "Sorry to interrupt," Nurse Irma said, looking from me to my grandfather. "I just wanted to remind Franklin that bingo starts in twenty minutes. I know he likes to get a good seat and they are filling up fast."

"Damnit Seraphina, you made me forget with all this skipping down memory lane." Pops stood and I reached out, grabbing his arm to help him as he shuffled to the bathroom closing the door.

Ending the recording on my phone, I stuffed my note journal and pens into my backpack.

"Did you have a good visit?" Nurse Irma asked, returning the chair Pops was sitting in to a small desk in the corner.

"Yeah, he was in a good mood today." I slung my backpack over my shoulder. Pops reentered the room. It looked as if he'd run a comb through his salt and pepper hair and he smelled like the fragrance counter at Macy's. "I thought you were going to bingo? Why the smell good?"

"Can't a man take pride in his appearance?" Pops asked, checking himself out in the mirror, which was in need of a spray of Windex.

"If I didn't know better I'd say you had a little girlfriend." I teased. It wouldn't surprise me in the least if he did. Grandpa Franklin had always been a ladies' man. He was married four times to three different women. And I'd seen the pictures from back in the day, Pops was Harry Belafonte fine.

"Girl hush I got bingo games to win." He reached for his cane and started toward the door.

Dropping him off at the recreation room, I kissed his cheek. "See you next Sunday."

"I look forward to it," he said, with a pat to my sepia cheek. I lingered at the entrance as he slowly made his way into the rec room. Nurse Irma was right, these old folks did not play when it came to bingo.

Before heading out I decided to grab a cold drink from the vending machine down the hall. Our normally mild, Michigan summers had reached record temperatures making it hot as hell. It didn't help that my little Toyota Corolla only knew how to blow hot air. With a thirty-minute ride back to Royal Oak I would be a sweaty mess by the end of it.

Approaching the vending machine, I stopped in my tracks. A mountain of a man was cursing and banging on the snack machine. Honestly, if this giant of a man used a bit more force, he could probably Hulk smash the hell outta that machine.

"You fucking piece of shit," he yelled banging on the glass.

"Did the machine just swipe your dollar?" I asked.

"It swiped five dollars and it won't drop my chips or give me my money back," he said, not bothering to turn in my direction, still yelling at the machine like it would feel sorry for him and stop holding his chips hostage.

Who puts five dollars in a vending machine? Moving forward I said, "These machines are sneaky bastards. You just have to know how to outsmart them."

The man looked at me like I was a homeless person begging for change. It made sense how he could think that, my kinky-curly hair was piled like a pineapple on top of my head. I wore loose, ripped jeans and a T-shirt with Steve Urkel from Family Matters on it making the, "Did I do that" face.

"Could you scootch?" I asked, pointing my finger to the right. He obliged, allowing me to work my magic. I smashed the buttons, hit the coin-return knob and swung my ample hips into the front of the glass. Like sorcery, coins spilled out of the machine and a bag of chips, a Clark Bar, and a pack of gum fell from their slots.

"Uhh ... that was impressive," he said as he bent to collect his quarters.

I took a bow before returning to the soda machine dropping four quarters in for a can of Coke.

"Here you go." He held out the candy bar and gum.

"No, you keep them."

"No, I just wanted the chips you should have the extra." He smiled, displaying a perfect row of teeth.

"OK, you ain't gotta tell me twice." *I'm not gonna turn down free shit,* I thought while stuffing the new-found goodies into the small zipper compartment of my backpack.

"I'm August, by the way." He extended his arm.

"Seraphina." With a smile I slipped my hand into his massive appendage.

"Nice to meet you. Do you come here often, Seraphina?" August asked, still gripping my hand.

"To the old folks' home ... yes actually." I chuckled. "My grandpa lives here. What about you? What brings you to Summercrest Senior Living?"

"My mother was recently admitted." He looked around the space. "This is my first time here actually."

"Well, it's one of the better facilities. Every place has problems but the staff at Summercrest seem to actually care about the residents. Which allows me to sleep at night."

"Yeah, I guess so." He rubbed the back of his thick neck.

"It was nice meeting you, August. Thanks for the snacks." Tapping my bag, I headed toward the door.

"Maybe we'll see each other again." August called out.

"I'm here every Sunday so ... it's possible." I tossed him one last curious glance before walking through the sliding doors.

SERAPHINA

ENTERING THE HOUSE, I exhaled a sigh of relief as the cool breeze of the air conditioning circulated all around. My T-shirt was soaking wet and even my toes felt sticky in my Converse sneakers. That's how hot it was outside. Since the start of summer, the extreme heat could only be compared to taking a road trip through hell. Dropping my backpack on the floor by the stairs, I sloshed to the kitchen. Opening the freezer, I stuck my head inside.

"You're back," my father, Herman, said from behind.

"I am." My head never moved from the icy air of the freezer.

"How was Pops?"

Grabbing some ice cubes, I closed the door. "He was good. Asked for you."

"Did he?" Dad's eyebrows hiked up his forehead. "I thought he was too busy being mad."

"He was never mad, he was hurt," I said, dumping the handful of ice into a glass followed by water from the jug.

"Well, I'm glad you had a good visit."

"I told Pops maybe next time you'll come with me." Taking a sip of the refreshing ice water, I sized him up.

"Maybe," he said. He'd been saying maybe ever since Pops was admitted to Summercrest seven months ago. Things between my father and Pops had been strained since Dad made the difficult decision to place Pops in a home. Pops was mad and he gave my dad an earful. The plan was for Pops to stay with my parents until he was called home, but that plan went bust when Pops became too difficult to manage on our own.

"I'm heading up." With a reassuring pat to his back, I took to the stairs.

After a cold shower I lay across my bed in a damp towel. If you told me a year ago I would be living with my parents again I would have called you a bald-headed liar. But here I was, laid out on my childhood bed in the house I grew up in. Adulting is hard and she hits like a linebacker.

After graduating from the University of Michigan I took a job as a freelance journalist working my way up. Before long I was being hired by some major media outlets, Essence magazine, The Village Voice and Vogue just to name a few. The ride was fast and exhilarating and I was shortsighted, leasing an apartment in New York I couldn't afford.

When the ride screeched to a halt, I was over one-hundred-thousand dollars in debt, in my defense that was mostly school loans. But my debt-to-income ratio was fucked and so was I. So here I was in my early thirties with parents as my roommates, or maybe they were more like my landlords.

My cell phone buzzed and shook on the bed next to me. Feeling for it, I unlocked the screen to find a text message from my cousin and best friend, Junie.

Junie: You coming out tonight?

Me: I have work tomorrow.

Junie: You'll always have work. That shit will always be there but your good fucking years are just passing you by.

Me: No.

Junie: Bitch you're going.
Me: Junie you know how my parents get.
Junie: Then just stay at my place tonight.
Me: OK, but we have to be home at a reasonable hour.
Junie: Bet.

Junie was like the little devil on your shoulder encouraging you to make poor decisions. When we were in high school, I wanted to go cruise the mall while Junie wanted to cruise the streets in a car that wasn't ours. Our parents had to pick us up from jail after we crashed someone's Honda Accord into the collision barriers along the freeway. She was always coming up with some hair-brained scheme that could potentially land us in jail or in a cooler at Clauson's Funeral Home. But tonight, I was serious we'd have a few drinks and then head straight home so I could get some much needed sleep.

THE LOCAL DIVE bar was packed for a Sunday night. I guess I wasn't the only one hoping to drink my cares away. My eyes panned the dimly lit bar which was blasting XYZ Baby over the speakers. No DJ just the same tired playlist on repeat. This neighborhood was the type of place where everyone knew everyone because we'd all gone to school together.

There was Chantel, the resident slut. OK, that was harsh but she did sleep with my high school boyfriend so she kinda deserved it. In the corner next to the jukebox that didn't work was Montrell, the first guy I ever dry humped. Good times. What I wouldn't give for a little dry hump action right about now.

Truthfully, I was craving more than a jean jam. I can't remember the last time I spread my legs wide and let it all loose. Based on the slim pickings in the bar, I would go back to

Junie's place, buzzed and unsatisfied. Living with one's parents was definitely a mood killer. But, even though I was in a bit of a slump I wasn't interested in fucking Booger Byron. We called him that because he used to eat his boogers in third grade. I'm sure he'd outgrown that practice by now.

My eyes settled on the area at the back of the bar where the dart boards hung in a row. A huge figure towered over all the rest. *How the hell had I missed him?*

Junie was busy flirting with David Fosco, a white boy she dated on and off. I think the switch was currently resting in the on position for those two. They were horrible together but Junie's memory was short because she was always willing to give him another chance. I warned her on more than one occasion about David but she didn't listen, so I decided to shut my mouth and let her do her. When he pissed her off, or worse, broke her heart again, I'd be there to pick up the pieces.

I pulled at Junie's sleeve. "Who's that tall brother by the dart board?"

Junie squinted in the general direction. "Doesn't look familiar."

She was as blind as a bat, but refused to wear her glasses when we were out at night. Everyone knew she wore glasses, but she said her glasses didn't match her thot attire. Junie turned her attention back to gap-toothed David. I guess I would have to be my own wingman tonight. Downing my Corona, I took the long way to the back of the space making sure to fluff my curls and deslick my t-zone on the way.

"I got next." I said to the man who was pulling darts from the board. *Please don't be ugly. Please don't be ugly.*

"Sure." He turned, fixing his gaze on my five-foot-four frame. "I know you."

"August, right?" I furrowed my brow realizing my chance at some much needed dick was the dude from Summercrest.

"Yep. And you?"

"Seraphina." I reminded him.

"I knew your name."

"No, you didn't."

He smirked. "You're right, I forgot your name. Not really sure why I lied about that."

"Human nature. It's cool."

August's big hands shuffled the darts from one palm to the other.

"So, you wanna play against me?"

"Yes."

"Then we should get you some darts. They rent them at the bar."

"I already have my own." I pulled out a red case with my customized darts inside from my back pocket.

"You just walk around with your own pair of darts?" He narrowed his eyes, sizing me up.

"Doesn't everyone?"

He shook his head. "Wow, I'm about to get my ass handed to me, aren't I?"

"Yes." I smiled, removing my crossbody purse and tossing it on a nearby table.

After three games, in which I won each one, August threw in the towel.

"You're really good." The dip in his chin signaling surrender.

"I was just lucky."

"Don't do that shit."

My eyebrows mashed together into a frown. "What?"

"Don't act like you didn't just whoop my ass."

With a hitch of my shoulders I said, "Sorry, force of habit. Most guys can't handle when a woman is better than them at anything."

"Oh, you're talking about them weak ass brothers who feel threatened by accomplished women."

"Yeah … men." I joked, amusement rippling my abdomen.

"I'm not one of *those* men."

"Hmm, OK." His arm brushed against mine as I swept past him. It was brief but a ribbon of arousal twirled inside me. Pulling my orange-tipped darts from the board, I placed them back in their case.

"Let me buy you a drink."

"You already bought me two."

"OK, let me buy you some wings." He pointed to a window that was connected to the kitchen and was still taking orders even though it was past midnight.

"The wings here are overpriced."

"Alright." August slid his hands into the pockets of his jeans. "Then what can I do for you?"

If I were a different type of woman, a confident, empowered woman, this would be the part where I told him he could use those lips of his to suck and bite on my nipples until they were taut and erect and slick with his spit.

"I could use some water." Heat invaded my skin. His half smile made it difficult to focus on anything else. It appeared he was happy to be given a task.

"One water coming right up."

August's hand found mine as he led me through the crowd to the bar. His grip was strong and the palms of his hand were rough and calloused. His strong hand had my mind wondering what it would feel like to be wrapped in his arms with his hands cupping my ass. After securing two bottles of water, we made our way outside. The bar was still packed and even though the AC was on full blast all the bodies were making the temperature rise.

"So, what are the odds of seeing you twice in one day?" I asked, twisting the cap off my water bottle.

"I don't know. For a minute I thought maybe you were stalking me."

"Really?" I snorted out a laugh. "Why exactly would I do that?"

August ran his hands over the space in front of his well-toned body.

"Oh, so because you're attractive you think I would stalk you?"

His eyebrow raised. "So, you think I'm attractive?"

"Mildly, don't let that shit go to your head."

A crowd exited the bar and August stepped closer so the rowdy group didn't pass between us. His chest was in my face so I got a good whiff of his gray T-shirt that smelled of laundry detergent. When we were playing darts, I noticed he had a super clean scent about him. Like bar soap, dryer sheets and fresh water deodorant.

"I think you're attractive too, not mildly. Extremely."

My heart did cartwheels in my chest. There was something behind his hooded eyes I couldn't identify but the way his gaze moved from my face, to my lips, before lingering on my breast caused my knees to soften as I tried to maintain my balance.

"How long have you been in Michigan?" I thought it best to shift the conversation so I could tamp down the nagging desire to shove my tongue down his throat.

"Most of my life. I was in Atlanta for a few years but I just moved back."

"And I've never seen you before today?" I shot him a dubious glance from the corner of my eye.

"I grew up in Farmington Hills and went to private school for most of it."

So, he was handsome and smart. He sucked at darts but still two out of three wasn't bad.

"What's your last name?" This was the part where I interrogated him a bit to make sure we didn't have any mutual connections. Like if I'd already slept with his brother or uncle I'd like to know now.

"Gardner."

My eyes lit up recognizing the name. "Do you have a sister named Janette?"

"Uh-oh, yes."

"I know her. We work in the same building. We're more like acquaintances. Janette's good peeps."

"I'm kinda impartial but yeah, she is." He cocked his head to the side with a lift of his chin. "Did I pass the test?"

Placing my hand on my hip I asked, "What test?"

"The test to determine if you're willing to continue entertaining me."

A blush tickled up the back of my neck before traveling to my cheeks, but luckily my mahogany skin tone concealed that fact. "For now, but there could always be a pop quiz."

Junie came stumbling out of The Red Cup with David close behind. "There you are. Girl, I've been looking for you. David and I are going to head back to my place."

"But you said I could spend the night?" My mouth pressed into a crinkled line.

"And you still can."

I grabbed Junie's arm pulling her aside. "I don't wanna listen to you and David fuck all night." Been there done that, and I had no intentions of tossing and turning all night while Junie put on a show calling David daddy and telling him he was the best she'd ever had.

"OK girl, then you can spend the night some other time."

I looked at my phone and it was almost one in the morning.

I couldn't come home this late, my parents would flip. Just the thought of them scolding me like I was a teenager who broke curfew made my stomach turn.

David came over interrupting our conversation. "You ready baby?"

Ugh, I hated this man. If he got hit by a bus, I wouldn't shed one tear. He's a toxic, manipulative fuckboy. And unfortunately, he had my cousin wrapped around his finger, or more accurately his dick.

"I've been ready." Junie thrusted her hips against his.

"Junie, how am I supposed to get home?" She was my ride.

"Call a fucking car service." David spit out the words.

One day I was going to slap the shit outta this man. Open handed, swinging from the back, using all my weight to bitch slap the taste out of his mouth.

"I can drive you home." August stepped forward.

I looked up at him like a deer caught in headlights. But before I could object, Junie chimed in. "Great, it's settled. Text me so I know you made it home OK."

And just like that she left me with a stranger at a bar. August could be a serial killer and Junie just handed me right over to him. She'd been my instant best friend since my aunt Louisa had her thirty-one years ago, but our friendship was often one sided with Junie selfishly doing whatever the fuck she wanted.

"I don't need you to drive me. I can call a RideX." Retrieving my phone from my purse, I opened the app. Any buzz I'd achieved was gone and now I was sober, pissed, and horny. I just wanted to go home, have my parents cuss me out and go to sleep.

August placed his hand over mine obstructing my view of the phone screen. "Really it's not any trouble."

Maybe I was being a little too rash. I had this fine ass man in front of me. And he was obviously interested, even if he moved slower than a tortoise. With a resigned breath I thought, fuck it. There was no reason this night had to be an entire bust. "Do you wanna have sex?"

He coughed on the sip of water he just took. "What?" His eyebrows steadily climbed his forehead.

"Sex, with me." I pointed at my chest in hopes of clearing up any confusion.

"Yes." His eyes were once again hooded and he advanced closer like I was gonna let him do me right here pressed against the side of the building.

"Can we do that at your place?"

"Yes." He stared at me for a long time, clearly speechless at how forward I was.

"Are we gonna go?"

"Oh my God ... yeah, of course. I'm parked over there." He pointed to a blue Chevy Nova.

"Great, let's do this."

three

SERAPHINA

AUGUST STOPPED the Chevy in front of a single-family home. Exiting the car, I walked up the drive making my way to the front door. August whistled causing me to stop in my tracks.

"I'm actually in the back."

With a bend to my waist, I looked toward the back of the long driveway. "You live in the garage?"

His broad shoulders hunched forward. "Yeah, is that a problem? Cause if it is I totally get it." August turned walking back toward his car. "Listen, this is a bad idea, I should just take you home."

"I live with my parents." I called out. Sure, I wasn't expecting a garage but I wasn't one to judge when I was staying with my mommy and daddy.

"So, you don't mind?" His face was hopeful.

"Not if you don't."

"Come on," he said, walking back toward the backyard, a noticeable pep in his step.

The garage had been converted into a studio apartment. It was cozy but functional, and more importantly it was his own space. Not gonna lie, I was lightweight jealous. The thing I

17

missed the most since moving back home was privacy. Last week I was in my room and my mom just barged in. No courtesy knock, just the door opened and then she was in my room touching my things. I loved my mother but boundaries weren't her strong suit.

August moved around the space, throwing a pile of clothes from the couch into a nearby closet.

"This place is nice." I offered.

"It's temporary. Like I said I just moved back to town. So, I'm still getting myself established."

"I get it." Another thing we seemed to have in common was our distaste for our respective living situations.

"Do you want some juice or water?"

"I'll take water and a bathroom if you have one."

"Yeah, right behind you," he said before turning to the small kitchenette.

In the bathroom I peed for what had to be two minutes straight. The space was modern but cramped. My knees were practically touching the wall. I wondered how August maneuvered in this tight space. After washing my hands, I snooped in the medicine cabinet to make sure there weren't any half-empty bottles of antibiotics.

His face lit up when I reentered the room. I guess I can't blame him, this random woman he'd only met today had agreed to have sex with him. Shit, I'd be sporting a goofy smile too.

Handing me a cold glass of water, he leaned against the counter. "So, you live with your parents. How's that going?"

"It's like a slow death." I chuckled, removing my crossbody purse and placing it on his two-seater dining table. "Don't get me wrong I love my parents but they're old school. Like curfews, and chores, and no locked doors. They don't give a fuck that I'm a grown woman. I'm under their roof so I must obey their rules."

"I'm guessing they would frown at you coming home at one in the morning."

"If by frown you mean a verbal tongue lashing. Then yes."

"Look, if the only reason you suggested coming home with me was to escape your parents' wrath, then—"

"That wasn't the reason I suggested it." I flashed him my best seductive gaze, but being sexy on cue wasn't my strong point.

"I'm just saying you're free to crash here, no strings attached."

Biting my bottom lip, I asked, "Are you always this polite?"

He rubbed the back of his neck with his hand. "You say it like it's a bad thing."

"It's not. But at this moment I'm not really looking for polite."

August worked the bottom half of his face into a frown. "What are you looking for?" His eyes tripped down the length of my frame.

"I don't know. Maybe your hand ... gently applying pressure around my neck."

August's eyes flickered and in a flash he crossed the room and scooped me off my feet. He used his massive arm to balance my ass before his lips descended onto mine. Reality as I knew it dimmed as our lips moved as one accord. It was as if his kisses were a vortex to another dimension and I was being sucked in. Frantic and longing, he searched my mouth with his tongue.

Depositing me on the bed he pulled off my high-top, floral print Converse sneakers before helping me out of my jeans. My eyes pinged from one rippling muscle to another as he pulled his shirt over his head, tossing it aside, revealing what I already knew. This man was a behemoth, with muscles flexing across his chest and arms. He looked like an urban lumberjack. That was the only way to describe him.

Removing my top, I cursed myself under my breath. Why was I always so ill prepared? I had plenty of sexy underwear that accentuated my positive, physical attributes. Mesh and see-through numbers with embroidered flowers. Demi bras that made it appear as if my modest B cups runneth over. But what did I wear tonight … cotton panties and a sports bra.

August didn't seem to mind as he removed his jeans. It was impossible to ignore the well-defined bulge in his boxer briefs. My heart leaped at the confirmation he was indeed big every-where. Standing to my knees I helped him remove his boxers, grabbing a hold of him. An audible gasp escaped my mouth as I held the weight of him in my hand.

Licking my palm, I slid my hand back and forth over his length. His breathing elevated as I spat onto it increasing my friction. Placing his hand on my shoulder, he applied pressure. My eyes darted to his face to ensure he was enjoying this as much as I was. I loved watching men react to my touch. It made me feel powerful and in control. This feeling didn't last for too long, August pushed me back aggressively, almost knocking the wind out of me.

"I'm sorry. Are you OK?" His face was riddled with concern.

"Yeah, I'm good." I rubbed my shoulder.

"I'm sorry, but if you kept doing that it was gonna be a very disappointing night."

He reached for the waist of my full-coverage panties and I hoisted my hips so he could pull them off with ease. My legs sprang open as if on hinges signaling I was ready and willing. His long arms reached for me and he grazed his middle finger over the folds of my vagina. It was brief but his touch forced me to cry out. I wanted him to fill me up but it appeared he wanted to tease me first.

Leaning in, he met my waiting mouth before making his way down my neck. Stopping at my sports bra he helped me remove it, his lips finding the curve of my breast. As his tongue sucked and teased one breast, his hand gently massaged the other. August's hand completely covered my B cups, his fingers flicked and pinched my nipple before rubbing the taut tip with his coarse palm. The rough touch against my soft skin was a nonsensical mixture of pleasure and pain.

His lips found their way back to mine and I sucked his lower lip into my mouth. August's left hand also moved on, landing in between my thighs. He ran a finger over my cleft like before, but this time his finger slipped inside. I moaned against his mouth as his long finger searched me. Pulling out, he ran his slick, wet finger over the outer edge of my vagina.

His touch initially slow and gentle, only to build in intensity caused my breathing to increase as gurgled moans tumbled from my throat. Just when I thought I couldn't take anymore he'd slipped two or three fingers inside of me causing me to regroup. His thumb swept across my bud, forcing my whole body to tense. His pace rhythmic and consistent.

"Please don't stop." I cried out.

"Do you like that?" He whispered; his eyes locked on my contorting face.

"Yes."

"I can tell. You're ruining my sheets." he teased.

"I'm sorry." I could barely muster the words.

"No need to apologize." He pulled away, lowering himself off the bed and plunging his face in between my thighs.

His wet tongue methodically stroking my most sensitive parts was too much for me to handle. From the slurping and moaning noises he made, it was clear he relished satisfying me. The sounds of him enjoying the feast that was Seraphina sent me over the top. A wave cresting higher and higher until it crashed down in a warm, tingling rush. His mouth was still roaming my chasm drinking in every last drop. The rapid beating of my heart played a melody in my ear, as my nerve endings fired with each pass of his tongue. I had to not so gently hit the top of his head to get him to release me.

Once he did all I could say over and over again was, "Oh God. Oh my God."

August stood, licking me from his face and hands before opening the drawer of his night stand, pulling a condom out and opening the seal. I stared with anxious eyes as he rolled the latex over his member. Truthfully, I wasn't sure I could handle another August induced orgasm, but I wasn't a quitter and I was eager to return the favor. He offered a skewed grin as he looked at me like he knew something I didn't. Closing my eyes, I gripped the bed sheets as he slowly entered me.

"Are you OK?" He stopped to ask.

"Uh-huh." I managed to nod focused on breathing.

With my meek reassurance, he finished his slow slide until he was snuggly in place. Grabbing my hips, he began to thrust, each one deeper than the last. It was as if the wind was knocked out of me. Once I regained my breath all I could do was cry out for him.

"August, fuck." I clawed at his arms. My eyes locked onto his face, August was biting his lip with focused determination as he rocked his hips back and forth.

After a few more minutes of this he pulled out. "Turn around." His voice was lower than normal, almost guttural.

I complied without hesitation, positioning myself for him, back arched, legs wide, arms stretched above my head. August gave my ass a firm slap causing my knees to quiver before reentering me. He just stood there completely surrounded by my love. *What was he waiting for.* I rocked over his length no longer able to wait. My backside reverberated against him before pulling away only to slam down on his shaft once more.

He didn't touch me, letting me do all the work. All I could hear was his faint breathing in between my murmured grunts. When he finally touched me, he fulfilled my wish wrapping his hand around the back of my neck. Grabbing my right hand, he placed it behind my back, pinning me in place. Leaning in, he was fully in control all I could do was receive each and every thrust. Burying my face into his bed sheets, I groaned as my body hummed with intense rapture.

I felt like Goldilocks after stumbling over Baby Bear's belongings, cause everything he was doing was just right. The fact I feared he'd be too gentle made me laugh out loud. This man was disrespectful, violating me in the best way. He seamlessly flipped me onto my back driving in once more, this time he hovered over me. His strong arms held him up so he didn't crush me. But I needed to feel his weight on top of me, grabbing his neck I pulled him closer. Our lips made contact and the taste of his tongue was intoxicating.

I wrapped my leg around his waist. I'd grown accustomed to his girth and now wanted him to plunge deeper to uncharted territory. He obliged with a thrust so intense I saw stars floating before my eyes. I grabbed his face in disbelief. *Where has this man been hiding?* Nice men with good dick were not as easy to find as you might think. August was a nice guy and the dick ... the dick was impeccable. Five-star rating. No scratch that, I didn't want the word to get out about him. I wanted this man all to myself. At least for the next few hours.

Heat flooded my center as his tongue teased my breast. It was his moaning in my ear that initiated the final eruption. My body shivered, my legs shaking as my eyes rolled into the back of my head. After a few more thrust, August groaned loudly, digging his hand into my thigh before collapsing next to me.

We lay there in silence, our faces flush in the afterglow. Just the sound of our breathing returning to normal and a clock ticking. August jumped up heading to the bathroom. I had to force myself to keep my eyes open for fear I'd fall fast asleep. Usually, I had difficulty sleeping at night because that was the time my brain wanted to replay all my awkward interactions or missed opportunities. But in this moment, all the competing thoughts that normally tumbled around my head were silent.

When August returned he handed me a warm washcloth. Apparently, the gentleman was back to close out the night. "Are you thirsty?" he asked.

"Yes." My throat was dry from all the panting and screaming. August added fresh cold water to our glasses, handing me one. "What time is it?"

"A little after two."

Ugh. I had to be up in five hours. "I should call a car to pick me up."

August rubbed at his eyelids. "Are you crazy? It's two in the morning. Just stay here."

A frown settled over my face. "I don't wanna impose." Pulling on my panty and bra I looked for my tank top.

"Seraphina, you just ended my four-month sex drought. Stay."

I let out a big yawn. The thought of getting dressed and the subsequent fifteen-minute ride to my place was not as appealing as curling up in August's warm bed, maybe with his heavy arms wrapped around me. "OK. Which side?"

"Left." He pointed, turning off the lights.

Climbing under the covers, I set my alarm for thirty minutes earlier than normal which would give me time to head home, shower, and change before going to work.

August climbed in next to me tilting his neck from side to

side until there was a popping sound followed by a satisfied sigh. "Good night."

"Night."

He plunged his hand in my curls giving my scalp a strangely satisfying scratch. "I like to cuddle. Is that OK?"

"Yeah sure." My face was indifferent but inside I was beaming. August wrapped himself around me, within seconds he was out like a light. Settling in, I rested my head against his shoulder. As my lids grew heavy, I thought, this sure beats a night sleeping on Junie's hard ass futon.

AUGUST

WHAT WAS it about good sex that made you feel like a new man? You know how a basketball team would celebrate when they won a game after a long losing streak, that was me. I'd been shooting bricks for the past few months, but last night, with very little effort, my fortunes changed.

Seraphina left thirty minutes ago and the pep in my step was undeniable. A morning person I was not, but this morning I was fired up and ready to go. Normally I would need a large mug of coffee to transform into a functional member of society. But flash backs of Seraphina calling for me as I drove deeper into her wet pussy, was all the motivation I needed to power me through the rest of my day.

I'd offered to give her a ride home but she declined claiming she was good. I got the impression she wasn't into people doing stuff for her. Which was cool, I totally respected that, I was a bit of a loner myself. If I asked you for help it was because I'd exhausted every option. This was something I was working on, trying to accept asking for help wasn't a sign of weakness but strength.

After a quick shower, I headed to the shop. Upon returning

to Michigan, I landed a job as a mechanic at Arturo's Auto Rider. The hours were decent and the money was good, and I felt comfortable working with my hands. As a kid I was a tinkerer always taking shit apart to figure out how it worked.

In high school my side hustle was fixing peoples' electronics and they'd pay me cold, hard cash. Eventually, that love of fixing thing turned into auto repair. My dad had a classic 1967 Chevrolet Corvette Convertible. While he never let me drive it, we did work on it together most weekends. Sourcing new parts, restoring others. I remember how proud I felt when we were done knowing I had a hand in restoring that car to its former glory.

Working in Arturo's auto shop was temporary, like I told Seraphina I was still trying to get myself reestablished. A fact most women weren't checking for, they expected you to bring shit to the table. And while I had tons to offer, a stable job, reliable transportation, a clean and well-mannered demeanor, when she was bringing a masters or a six-figure income it was hard to compete. Most women wanted men who were on their level and right now I was kinda low. So, finding a woman who was willing to sleep with a dude who lived in a garage was refreshing. But she lived with her parents so maybe my situation was goals to her.

"Morning Arturo."

"It's gonna be another busy day. You have the silver Honda. Total engine overhaul."

I glanced out the large windows at the parking lot that was quickly filling up with cars. Setting up my station, I prepared for the day.

"Yo, how was your night?" Sylvester asked, with a hearty slap to my back. Sly was my coworker and we'd taken a fast liking to one another, often stopping for drinks after work. "Did you and ole girl end on a high note?" Sly was also at the bar with me last night and watched as Seraphina beat me in darts.

"Nah, I took her home. Then I went back to my place and crashed." I lied, Sly didn't need to know who I was smashing. It was a one-night stand, a much needed one-night stand. I could feel my penis jump just thinking about her plump, wet lips ... both of them. Before she left, she thanked me saying she had a good time. I was hopeful she'd be down to doing that shit again sometime soon.

Sly shrugged. "I get it, it's hard to get wet for a guy who plays darts as badly as you do."

"Whatever fool. It was late and I'm a gentleman."

"More like old fashioned." He handed me a stack of vehicle evaluation forms. "Look, you have no game. Women these days want a thug and you over here opening car doors and buying flowers."

"When did that shit become uncool?" I asked, pulling out my impact wrenches and setting them at my station.

"It's a new day my dude. People are just trying to get their rocks off. Ain't no one looking to settle down. Shit the females be worse than the men."

I sucked my teeth. "I don't believe that."

"Plus, ain't no woman trying to be laid up with your Andre the Giant looking ass. It probably costs half their pay check just to feed you three square meals a day." Sly joked.

Adding the evaluation forms to my clipboard I said, "We can't all be pocket sized like you."

"Bruh, I'm six foot." Sly straightened his back and planted his feet firmly on the ground hoping to grow a few inches.

"Nah, you're five eleven and that's me being generous." I patted the top of Sly's head before heading to the back to get batteries for my diagnostic scanner.

While I didn't appreciate Sly's grim take on the dating

scene, he wasn't wrong. Since being single it just seemed like people were looking for quick connections, no one was trying to plant roots. Which sucked for me because I was a gardener and was actively looking for a plot of land I could cultivate and call my own.

I wondered if Seraphina had a green thumb. It was difficult keeping my mind off her. When she left this morning, it felt real non-committal and I'd been rolling over in my head ways I could ask her out on a date and hopefully get her to rotate her hips against mine again. Luckily, I had an entire week to come up with some witty banter so we could turn that one night only into an encore performance.

OPENING the front door to my mother's house, the familiar scent of home wafted through my nostrils. "Yo, Janette where you at?" I called.

"I'm up here in Daddy's office." My sister's voice rang out.

I stopped at the door not wanting to cross the threshold. I hadn't been in that room since my dad passed over a year ago. "What are you doing?"

"Just packing up some of Dad's old things. He held onto the most random shit." Janette was two years older than me. I was the baby of the family and the only male with five older sisters.

"Did you visit Mommy like you promised?"

"I did." I leaned on the door jam my eyes resting on Janette who was sitting cross-legged on the floor, wrapping fragile items in course paper.

She tossed her long, ombre braids over her shoulder looking up at me. "What did you think?"

"Of?"

"Of the facility, Summercrest."

I lifted my shoulders with a blasé shrug. Janette knew I didn't like seeing my mom in that place. But I was outvoted five to one. Another reason having five older sisters sucked, they'd often team up against me. I suggested one of us move in and look after her. But because I was in Atlanta at the time I'd made that suggestion, it seemed to fall on deaf ears. It just felt wrong having a stranger look after the woman who changed my diapers and kissed my ouches better. That's why I'd moved back home, I was determined to get her out of Summercrest. How I was gonna make that happen was the piece I hadn't quite figured out yet.

"She's happy there and is really getting on well. Did she tell you that?" Janette asked.

"You know Mom, always spinning a sunny perspective onto even the worst situations."

Janette frowned. "It's not a bad situation. It was the best option."

"Was it?" Heat was creeping up my neck. "I still don't understand how throwing our mother into a home became our only option."

"What would you have had her do, tool around this big old house until she took a tumble or burned the place down?"

"You guys didn't even give my suggestion any weight. You just brushed it aside like y'all always do."

Janette stood stretching her frame to its full five-nine length. "Your suggestion was for someone to take care of her, but you weren't stepping up to the plate to volunteer as tribute."

My pulse ramped into a thundering stampede. "I was in Atlanta. I had a life there. I couldn't just up and leave."

"We all have lives, Auggie." Janette's gaze was fierce.

"Yeah well, I'm here now."

"A day late and a dollar short."

"Fuck you."

Janette rested her hands on her hips, impaling me with her cold gaze.

That look always sent chills up my spine. "I'm sorry. I didn't mean that."

"That's what I thought. You may be as big as a tree but you are not too old to get your ass whipped."

I raised a surly eyebrow. "By who?"

"Me, with one hand tied behind my back."

We shared a laugh at the thought of that. She was probably right, all my sisters were strong willed, independent, ass kickers. When the neighborhood bully was picking on me it was my sister Janette who threatened to rearrange her nose. Yes, my bully was a girl but in my defense, she was bigger than me at the time, my growth spurt wouldn't kick in until summer, and she was a girl.

We don't hit girls in the Gardner home. I learned the hard way when I was eight and hit my sister Kimberly. My dad laid into me and told me if I ever placed a hand on one of my sisters or any woman in violence, he would break my jaw. Did I mention I was eight?

Her shoulders relaxed as she changed the subject. "When am I getting an invite to your place?"

"My place is barely bigger than this room. Not really party central."

"I still wanna see it. I need to get you a housewarming gift. Do you have a plant? I bet you don't. I'll get you a plant."

"Please don't."

"Why? Plants are cool now."

"If you gift me a plant, its death will be on your hands."

"It takes two seconds to water and dust it."

"Nope, I don't want that kinda commitment. I can barely take care of myself."

"You could get your girlfriend to help you." Her statement was more of a question, casting a line to see if she got a bite. I didn't have a girlfriend and if I did, I wouldn't share that information with her. The family didn't get to meet the random women I dated. When I found my better half maybe I'd introduce them ... at the wedding.

"What are you doing with all this stuff?" I motioned my hand around the room.

"Mom and Dad just have so much crap. I get it, who doesn't have piles of stuff after living in a place for so many years, but damn."

"Does Mom know y'all are going through her things?"

"Well, someone has to. Dee's been sorting through all the paperwork and documents. She found a ton of old photos, art work, and report cards from when we were kids. They're in this box if you're interested." Janette kicked a banker box with her foot.

"Interested in what? Why are we sorting through Mom's things like she's ..." I stopped short. I didn't want my mother and that word uttered in the same sentence.

"August, that's not what this is. But if we're gonna sell the house we have to clear it out."

"Yeah, and speaking of that, why exactly are we selling the house?"

"We've been over this a million times."

"No, actually you guys decided, ignored my many objections and teamed up on me like you always have."

She discharged a grunted breath. "You were not going to be able to take care of Mom all by yourself."

"I could have." I lifted my chin challenging her words.

"You just said you don't want the responsibility of a house plant. I can guarantee you Mom is going to need more than the occasional dusting."

Speaking through my teeth with forced restraint I said, "Nette, that's different and you know it."

As the youngest, most of my sisters helped raise me. I think they all still saw me as the little kid who followed them around asking for one more story before bedtime. My mother always told me I could be anything I wanted. But in this family the one thing I could never be is respected as an adult. I loved my sisters but much of what I said was ignored, or even worse, dismissed. Which was why I chose to stay away most of the time.

"I don't want to fight about this, again."

Frustration gripped the muscles of my jaw. "Then let's not fight." Turning on my heels I bounded down the stairs.

"August, wait. You're acting like a baby." Janette followed yelling after me.

Her words had the intended effect stopping me in my tracks. I hated being called the baby. And she'd said that in the hopes I'd back down and give in but I was done allowing them to steam roll me.

Her tone shifted as her gaze softened on my face. "Can you just talk to me?"

"I've tried to talk to you but none of you will listen. So, I'm officially done, do whatever the fuck you want." The glass pane in the front door rattled violently from the force I exerted opening it. Maybe I was overreacting but all this shit was moving entirely too fast. Putting Mom in a senior care facility, the assortment of boxes scattered throughout my childhood home signaling the end, time needed to slow down. We just lost my father a year ago, I couldn't lose her too.

"OH MY, I thought for sure you'd be sick of me by now." My mother gushed at the sight of my face.

"Last Sunday, I told you I'd be back next week. Remember?" I kneeled so I could kiss her soft cheek.

"I remember, I thought *you'd* forget."

"How could I forget my favorite girl."

"Hmph, now I'm your favorite girl. When you were out in Atlanta you could barely return a call." She flashed one of her signature, stern-mother looks that always let me know my ass was grass.

"Only because I was busy. Not because I didn't care." This is how every conversation with my mother started. She would guilt me for being neglectful, for not returning calls, for taking my only mother for granted. I would reassure her. Tell her I loved her and patiently wait for her to move on to more pleasant topics.

She sucked her teeth. "Geesh, you only have one mother, you'd think a son would be more attentive."

"You're right. I'm sorry."

"Are you all settled into your new place?" She removed her reading glasses, giving me a thorough once over.

"Yep, I didn't come with much so moving in was pretty easy." I'd sold most of my things just moving my bed, couch and clothes, and a few personal belongings. The choice to move back home wasn't easy but when it became clear my siblings were serious about this old folk's home business, I knew I had to make a return.

By the time I was able to move back, my mother was already a resident of Summercrest. It took me a few months to muster the courage to make the trip out here. Summercrest Senior Living was in the city of Plymouth, roughly a thirty-minute drive from my place in Royal Oak. It wasn't the drive holding me back, it was having to see her in this place.

"What about you, how has this place been treating you?"

Janette claimed Mom was adjusting to her new living situation but I wanted to hear my mother affirm it.

"There are nicer rooms with bigger windows." She cast an eye to the standard-sized window in her room. Summercrest was set up like mini studio apartments. With a small living space, an area for a bed and end tables, and then a bathroom with handholds anchored to every wall and in the shower so residents had something to hold on to while making their way around.

This place looked just like the brochure Janette emailed to me months ago. Each resident had a private room. There were no kitchenettes, not even a microwave. If they wanted to eat, they headed down to the cafeteria. The seniors who were bed-bound got room service.

"Yeah, and those rooms with the nice big windows cost a shit-ton more." I cringed quickly correcting myself. "A lot more."

"When did you start cursing?"

"I don't curse." I only cursed occasionally and when I really needed to emphasize my point.

"Are your little friends telling you it's cool to have a potty mouth? I didn't raise you like that Augustine."

I chuckled at her words. She was the only one alive who still called me Augustine. As far as my friends were concerned, my God given name was August. Augustine was my father's name and it was just far too formal for a mechanic from Michigan.

"Yes ma'am. I'm sorry."

Pulling out a small TV tray I placed it between us. With little effort my mother shuffled the card deck. She was the best slap-jack player I'd ever gone against. Even when we were young, she played to win, Bernadette Gardner did not care we were kids. She didn't believe in letting children win as a boost of confidence. She always said, "No one is ever gonna hand anything to you, not even your momma."

At eighty-two her reflexes had slowed but she was still pretty damn good. She could no longer beat me but she was still a formidable opponent. One time I tried throwing several hands so she could win, and when she figured it out she cussed my ass out in the most Christian way possible. Since that day I played to win because I respected her and she didn't deserve me pandering. She handed the deck to me so I could deal the cards.

"You feeling lucky?" I asked.

"It's not about luck, it's about skills. Now deal them cards so I can whoop your behind."

AFTER THREE ROUNDS of cards with my mother we said our goodbyes. I lingered in the hall near the vending machines hoping to bump into Seraphina again. She'd been on my mind all week. Our unexpected escapade playing on a loop in my head, made it difficult to focus on anything else. There was also her smile. She had dimples on both cheeks and when she smiled it was the sweetest surprise.

"Nice to see you don't have trust issues." Her voice called from behind me. *How did I miss her coming?*

"What?"

"The machine, after last week's attempted robbery you're not holding a grudge."

"I guess my stomach is stronger than my pride. Plus this time I brought quarters." I flashed the coins in my hand.

"Don't mind me, I'm just getting a soda for the road."

"Do you wanna grab a coffee or something?" When I practiced this in my head this part went way smoother. I'd say something funny and she'd laugh, playfully twisting the curls in her soft hair. And then when I'd suggested coffee she'd one up me and ask for something stronger and then I'd fuck her in the backseat of my car.

She eyeballed me suspiciously. "I don't like coffee."

"OK … well … they have tea, or hot chocolate. Have you tried a Frappuccino you can get that without coffee? Or maybe a pastry, they have cookies and cinnabuns. Or if you prefer something savory, they have sandwiches, and like little snack boxes." I was rambling, she did not need for me to run down the menu offering at Bean There Done That.

"I could go for a large cup of water." She fanned herself with her hand.

"You're a cheap date." I chuckled. "I mean … this isn't a date … not at all. That's just an expression. I don't mean we're going on a date." At this point my arms were flailing and sweat was coasting down my back as I tried to retract my words. She must think I'm an idiot. "Not that I wouldn't go on a date with you. If that was something you wanted. But coffee isn't a date. It's just two people casually enjoying hot or cold beverages together." I took a much needed breath. "How much longer are you gonna let me flounder like this?"

Seraphina ducked her head with a smile. "I was just marveling at your ability to verbally spin your wheels."

Unlike me she didn't seem easily flustered, I liked that. I wore my feelings on my sleeve. If I was happy, you knew it. If I was mad you knew to stay away.

"So, are we gonna do this coffee, which is not a date, thing now?" I asked.

"Sounds like a plan."

My face lit up in recognition. "That's what I should've said before."

SERAPHINA

"SO, HOW OLD IS YOUR MOM?" I asked, biting into a piece of red velvet pound cake.

"Eighty-one … no scratch that she's eighty-two just had a birthday a few months ago."

"Whoa, she's almost as old as my grandpa." I blinked realizing that could be offensive. "Not that there's anything wrong with that."

"Nah, it's cool. I get it all the time. I was a … surprise. My mom was forty-seven. My dad was even older. They were not trying to have any more babies."

"What happened?"

"I don't know, maybe uncontrollable lust. I don't really like to think about my parents …" He smashed the palms of his large hands together. "You know what I mean."

I'd followed August to the coffee shop and after settling in with his coffee and my water we'd been playing twenty questions. While he grew up in Farmington Hills, he was bused to a predominantly white private school a county over from kindergarten to senior year. His favorite animal was the sloth, which was insane, but OK. And coffee was his drug of choice. If he could he would take an intravenous line of French roast straight to the veins. His words not mine.

"Was it a good visit?" I asked, wiping away cake crumbs from the table.

"Yeah, as much as it can be in a place like that. I'd prefer to visit with my mom in her kitchen and have her cut me a slice of her lemon Bundt cake, but Summercrest will have to do ... for now." He took a sip from his coffee which was a beige color after all the creamer he'd added.

"Sounds like Summercrest wasn't your choice?" Shifting in my chair, I leaned closer.

"Nope, that would be my sisters."

"How many sisters do you have?"

"Five, all older."

"That sounds fun. I would've loved to have a sister or two growing up. Do you know how hard it is to blame things on an imaginary friend when you're twelve?"

"Sometimes it was fun I guess, but most of my sisters are over ten years older than me. I'm closest to Janette cause we're just a few years apart."

"Do you see them often?"

"Janette, all the time. The others, mostly during holidays or funerals."

I bobbed my head in agreement. "Families can be complicated. And life gets so busy. I don't remember seeing that in the adulting brochure."

"Naw, it was all about staying up late, drinking, and being able to eat cold pizza in the middle of the night. They hid the real shit in the fine print."

"I never read the fine print."

"And that's how they get you." He wagged a finger in my direction.

I'd be lying if I said I wasn't happy to bump into August

again. Mostly because I was interested in his particular brand of physical therapy. I didn't have an addictive personality but this man and his dick could change all that.

August wiped at the corners of his mouth and beard with his napkin. "What about you? You mentioned you visit your grandfather. How long has he been there?"

"Almost a year. It's weird other than my dad, my grandpa was the strongest man I'd ever known. When I moved back home, he was different. I guess we all were, but he was slower, not always so sure about things. My parents moved him in to live with us and for a while it worked. It seemed like it was good for him having us around. But then one day he left the house while we were at work and he was missing for hours. It was then we knew we couldn't handle it ourselves anymore."

Chills touched my spine as I thought back to that day. My mother was frantic and Dad was concerned even though he tried to remain calm. I remember thinking if something happened to Pops I would never forgive myself. Instead of heading home after getting off work at three, I'd gone to happy hour with some friends. Maybe if I'd come straight home none of this would've happened. Pops would've never wandered off and my dad wouldn't have started seriously considering Summercrest.

"I'm sure that was scary as hell." August's face was lined with concern. He was a good listener. Listening was an art. Most people only pretended to listen, just waiting for their chance to speak again. In the thirty or so minutes we'd been at the coffee house, August allowed me to talk … a lot. Mostly about stupid, mundane stuff. Maybe he's more of the strong, silent type. "How'd your grandpa handle the transition?"

"Badly, he feels betrayed, like my dad just dumped him off. My grandfather's a prideful man so moving in with my parents was a fight. And being shipped to Summercrest was like the onset of World War III. Pops put up a fuss saying he didn't need looking after. I think he felt abandoned, sure he needed to be monitored but a home should be the last resort."

"Is that your grandfather speaking or you?" He took a sip from his coffee which I was certain had to be lukewarm now.

I chewed at my bottom lip. Perhaps, I was also holding onto some resentment surrounding my parents' decision. Throwing Pops into a senior facility was extreme. I just wished we'd taken time to explore all our options.

Scanning the lock screen on my phone, I asked, "Do you wanna get out of here?"

August's head gave a quick jerk. "Bored already?" He teased.

"Nope, the barista is just giving me the evil eye. I think we've overstayed our welcome."

"What do you wanna do?" He cracked his knuckles, leaning back in his chair.

I shrugged, "I don't know, maybe we could go back to your place." The thought of him inside of me gave me sharp palpitations.

His gaze explored my features. "And do what exactly?"

"Whatever you wanted." Fidgeting with the jade crystal charm dangling from my neck, I wondered what it was about him that made me so forward.

His face looked exactly as it had the first time I propositioned him.

August leaned in with a whisper. "Well, you could come over and sit on my face for a bit."

Did polite August Gardner just ask me to ride his face? Yes! I do. I will. It's all I've wanted. "Yeah sure," I said breathlessly. "Or we could watch a movie." I didn't want to come off as too eager.

AUGUST

WE DID NOT WATCH A MOVIE. Right now she was on top of me doing exactly what I asked. My tongue, stiff and extended as she rocked back and forth across my face. I let my hands roam from her waist, to her spine, finally landing on her perfectly round breast that jiggled as she gyrated.

Seraphina didn't seem interested in playing games. She wanted to be fucked and I had all the fucks to give. Her thighs tightened around my ears as she let out a moan that was both low and high at the same time. She climbed down from my face, her wetness landing on my basketball-short-clad lap. Even with that cloth of fabric between us I knew she could feel me. Her deep-set, mink-brown eyes were mellow with low lids, as if she'd just inhaled a long drag of weed. Leaning in, Seraphina kissed my lips. The thought of her tasting herself on my tongue made my dick hum with anticipation.

"You good?" I asked. "Are you ready for more?"

She nodded, biting her plump bottom lip. Gently pushing her off of me, I removed my shorts and donned a condom. Placing her on my lap once more, I helped her get situated on my shaft. Seraphina wrapped her arms around me as our bodies moved in time with one another. I squeezed her ass so tight I was sure it would leave a print. She leveraged her weight using my knees for balance as she rocked her hips.

Sinking into the couch cushions, I enjoyed the show. This woman was perfect, and I'm not just saying that because it had been a minute since I'd had sex. She was stunning. Her skin, smooth and soft with stripes strategically on her ass like it was an art installation. She had beads around her waist and I had to remind myself not to grab hold too tightly, for fear I might break them. And then there was the way she looked at me, like she appreciated every single thrust and every long stroke.

Standing I could feel her thighs lock around my waist. I took deliberate steps to the bed, placing her on the edge with ease. With one of her legs straight in the air flush against my chest I began to go to work. I wanted her to feel me, all of me, taking great delight in knowing the twitch in her leg, the rolling of her head from side to side, and her nails clawing into the fleshy meat in my arm, was all because of me.

"Whose pussy is it?"

She glared at me, lip trembling a defiant expression on her face. *Oh, she thinks this is a game.*

"Whose ... is ... it?" I asked again, this time following each word with a long deep thrust that caused her to gasp.

"Oh fuck, OK. It's yours." She murmured.

"Do you feel that?" I bent my knees slightly which made my next stroke more angled.

She nodded, her eyes unfocused as her hips worked to meet me.

Dropping her leg, I reached for her arms pinning them over her head, asking "Is this, OK?" I knew not every woman liked being pinned down and I just wanted Seraphina to enjoy this as much as I was.

"Yes," she squeaked out.

Clutching her wrist tighter, I climbed on top performing laps like an Olympic swimmer until our bodies tensed and then released almost in unison.

With her head resting on my arm I absentmindedly played with the colorful beads around her waist. I wanted to crawl under the covers and envelope her in my arms, my head buried in her mass of tight curls until we fell asleep. Before I could suggest we partake in a midday nap, with the hopes that when we woke up we could go for round two, Seraphina stirred next to me.

"I should go," she said, sitting up.

"I don't mind if you stay." I tried to keep the tone of my voice non-committal.

"I can't, it's my mom's birthday. There's gonna be cake." She stood searching for her clothes. Finding her bra, she fastened it pulling the straps over her shoulders.

"When can I see you again?" I asked, sitting up on the bed. No longer concerned with looking cool, I was ready to pen her name on my calendar in permanent marker, making every day Seraphina day if she let me.

"Who said we're doing this again?"

I tilted my head flashing her a skeptical mug. We both knew we were going to do this again.

Jumping into her ripped jean shorts, she placed her purse over her body. "Maybe I'll see you next Sunday?" She headed for the door still shoving her feet into her shoes. "Thanks for the sex, it was just what I needed."

"Glad I could be of service." My shoulders slumped due to her lack of enthusiasm. I wanted to fuck her again and I was hopeful, based on her vocal enjoyment just moments ago, she wanted to make that a reality. My thoughts recalled Sylvester's words the other day about people no longer being interested in long-term connections and his claim women were the worst, more concerned with a quick release and not a relationship.

"Bye." Seraphina hurried toward the door.

Jumping from the bed, I followed her down the drive. "Maybe we should exchange numbers?"

She looked back, her eyes growing wide as she observed my naked form. Which I just realized was flashing the entire neighborhood. Retreating, I ducked behind the door offering a bashful smile. "That way I could call you." I shouted after her. But she ignored me, hopping into her Toyota, which was in desperate need of a tune up, and driving away.

seven

SERAPHINA

"WELL LOOK what the cat dragged in," Junie said when I opened the front door to my home. "From the looks of it he drug you in from your hair."

Touching the curly coils piled atop my head, I did my best to fluff them back to life.

"Girl, where have you been? The party started over an hour ago."

"I was visiting Pops." Hanging my backpack from the banister I scanned the dining and living rooms. All the usual suspects were in attendance for some free food and spiked punch.

"All this time? Ugh, I know he is tired of you. That man is not a social butterfly."

Junie was right, Pops was a man of few words. But when you got him warmed up, gold would spill from his tongue. Stories about my dad growing up. Retellings of his courtship with my grandma Loretta, his second wife. My family wasn't big on living in the past; they were too busy trying to stay afloat and navigate the present.

"Traffic was also a bitch," I said, eyeing the ceiling because if I looked Junie straight on she would know I was lying.

Junie narrowed her eyes. "You know you're a bad liar, right?"

Correction, apparently Junie would know I was lying because she knew me better than anyone. She was right, I was terrible at lying. So, you can imagine how often I was grounded after coming home past curfew, never able to fully commit to whatever lie Junie and I cooked up. I grabbed her arm and pulled her into the half bath to the right of the stairs.

"OK, I was with August."

"Who?" Junie admired herself in the mirror.

"August, the dude from the bar last Sunday."

"You mean the brother that stood head and shoulders above everyone else in the place?" Her face lit up.

I already knew what she was about to say. You know the saying about finding a nice guy and settling down? Well, Junie wanted me to find a guy, preferably one who was willing to do the freak nastiest stuff and then act the fool.

Falling for some guy was the last thing I needed right now. My life was out of control. I was virtually hurtling through space with my oxygen reserve at five percent. How could I focus on another person and making them happy when I couldn't even secure my own happiness?

"Yes, the tall dude."

"Seraphina Jacobs, are you fucking the Jolly Green Giant?"

"No," my normally deep voice raised several octaves. "No, we are not."

With a robotic voice Junie responded. "Lies detected."

"OK, we only did it once."

Junie sucked air through her teeth.

"Twice. That's it and it's not happening again." The way she could read me like a book was maddening. Maybe it was a blessing I didn't have any sisters because Junie was more than enough.

"Why not?"

"Because I have bigger fish to fry. If you hadn't noticed I'm currently living with my folks. I need to fix that ASAP."

"I know the girl who was on the track team, editor of the school newspaper, and a part of the chess club isn't afraid of a little multi-tasking?"

"In high school. This real-world shit ain't nothing like Clawson High School. Life hits a whole lot harder."

"We both can agree you got knocked on your ass but ain't shit changed, you're still the hard working overachiever I've always known. This too shall pass or whatever Shakespeare said."

I hitched my shoulder. Have you ever stopped at a train crossing waiting for the train to pass by? That was my life. I was waiting at a crossing and this never-ending train was zooming past. I couldn't turn around because there was a line of cars behind me and I couldn't pull forward because of the train. I was stuck. For the past year I'd been stuck at this train crossing and the funny thing was, I had no guarantees what was on the other side of these railroad tracks was any better.

"So, while you're waiting why not entertain Mr. Too Tall and Too Thick." She raised a curious eyebrow. "He thick right? Cause he looks like he's thick."

I flashed her a smile but the details of Mr. Gardner's physical prowess was something I was keeping to myself.

There was a knock on the door. "Are you almost done in there? I gotta pee." It was Kimmy, our baby cousin.

Unlocking the door, we stepped out. "It's all yours," I said.

Kimmy scurried in, closing the door behind her. In the living room was where the party was in full swing. All of my grandpa's kids and their kids in one room. When you stop to think about family and how we come together, it really is awe-inspiring. Two people meet and fall in love and their love creates this, a room full of people all connected because two people find one another and decided to give forever a try.

"There she is." My mother called as Junie and I entered the room.

Making the rounds I said my hellos, handing out hugs, kisses, and secret cousin handshakes where appropriate. I saved the birthday girl for last, throwing my arms around her, we rocked side to side. It was all extra because I'd burst into my parent's room at seven o'clock this morning, and sang the Stevie Wonder version of "Happy Birthday" at top volume. Some things never changed. I'd been doing that since I was a little girl, and even when I was living in New York I would call and sing to her over the phone.

"Happy Birthday," I whispered in her ear, planting a kiss on her ageless cheek. "Should I get the fire extinguisher for the candles on the cake just in case?" I teased.

"You are not that far behind me." She poked me in my ribs.

My mom wasn't lying. Today marked her forty-eighth birthday. She had me when she was fifteen. That was one of the reasons my parents were so strict. They didn't want me making the same mistake they had. Their attempt to protect me had more of a smothering effect, sending me looking for the fastest ticket out of the city. When I'd reluctantly returned home, trust me if I had any other options I would not have, my parents gravitated to the same parenting style they used when I was a teenager. No nuance, no taking into consideration the fact that I was thirty-three, just rules and punishment.

My father entered the living room carrying a sheet cake from the local grocery store ablaze with candles. We all broke out in a church rendition of "Happy Birthday" complete with a praise dance from Uncle Alvin. Canvassing the room landing on all the faces that looked like mine filled me with joy. I knew this feeling would be short-lived, quickly replaced with fear, despair, and a hearty dose of self-loathing, but I was going to bask in the shiny, warm glow for as long as I could.

eight

AUGUST

PACING outside the store front I waited for Sly. This dude could never be on time, which pissed me off. I believed in punctuality, if you were on time you were late. When we got off work, he was supposed to be right behind me. It was only a fifteen-minute drive. Finally, his truck parked next to my Nova and he exited the vehicle, specialty coffee in hand.

"You stopped for coffee?" I barked.

"Chill, I got you one too." He extended his hand offering me a cup.

I accepted, inhaling the nutty-mocha roast poured over ice. Coffee could fix almost anything. Having a bad day, grab a cup. Lost your job, a steaming-hot cup of joe could fix that. Found out your girlfriend is cheating on you with your best friend, grab a cold brew before you head over there and beat his ass.

"Thanks." I said, pointing to the vacant building. "So, what do you think?"

"I think this place should be condemned." Sly's head pivoted as he scanned the building.

"I know it looks rough—"

"Rough, this looks like the land that time forgot."

I held up my hand to silence him. "It's rough, but the inside is elite. Clean, well laid out, all the shit we'd need to hit the ground running and open our own shop."

"I don't know Gus, this area is sketch."

I knew he would say this but I'd done my research and this part of the city was seeing a sort of renaissance. I'm not talking about gentrification, where white people flood a predominantly black neighborhood, eventually pushing anyone who doesn't fit a certain aesthetic out. No, this was a resurgence. New, minority-owned businesses were popping up every day. In a year, maybe two, this neighborhood would catch up and our business could only grow from there.

After relaying all this to Sly, we went inside for the tour. The real estate agent was thorough, pointing out all the features and reiterating what I'd told Sly outside about the revitalization.

"This place was an auto shop before it closed. So, it's already outfitted for us. All we have to do is clean it up. Maybe install some tempered windows and we are golden." I offered.

"What happened to the previous owner? Did he close because business was slow?"

"No, he died. This shop is surrounded by homes. Those homes have cars that need oil changes and tune-up and eventually major repairs. We could handle all that. We would be the go-to shop in the neighborhood run by two brothers who look exactly like our customers, charging a fair price with fast repair times, and outstanding customer service."

Sly walked from one station to the other. "You really think we could do this?"

"I know we can."

Sly scrubbed his face with his hands. "Most businesses fail. You know that right?"

"We ain't gonna fail." Honestly, I had nothing to back that

statement up but my sheer will and desire, and the fact that failure wasn't an option. I needed this and I was willing to bust my ass, knock on doors, and engage in dreaded small talk to make this happen.

Sly released a resigned breath. "OK, let's sign the papers."

nine

SERAPHINA

"I GUESS I was an equal opportunity lover." Pops coughed out a laugh.

"So was Gran your one true love?" I'd had three different Grandmothers but Gran, Loretta Jacobs was my favorite. Probably because she's the one I grew up with. Loretta was Pops's second and fourth wife.

"Can't really put a label on something like that. Love is different depending on who you're with but if I'm being honest the one that got away holds a special place in my heart."

I leaned forward in my chair, with a quick glance to ensure my phone was still recording.

"The one that got away?"

"Yeah, she was the love of my life."

My eyes bulged wide at this declaration and the cavalier way Pops said it. Love of his life was a hefty title. Pops had been married four times but none of those women were his one true love?

"Wait, Grandpa, who are you talking about?"

"Bernie, when God made her he just phoned every other woman in there after. She was perfection. Shaped like them old

Coke bottles. You know the kind." Pops waved his hands into a curvy shape. "She was thicker than a bowl of porridge. We went to high school together. I was a few years ahead. She'd let me walk her home from school and sometimes we'd take a detour off the main street and she'd let me hold her hand." His face lit up at the recollection. "She had the softest hands, they were always able to soothe my restless soul."

"Was Bernie a nickname or her government name?"

"Everybody had nicknames back then. They called me Frankie or Frank.

"What was Bernie's last name?

"She had a few. When I got back from the war she'd married. You know I wrote her letters every week. One day I received a letter telling me she's marrying another fella. I've never been a crying man but I cried a few tears that night."

"So that was it. Your high school sweetheart married someone else while you were away." Didn't sound like much of a soul mate to me.

"She did. But when I returned home it seemed like she regretted that decision."

"How do you know?" I asked, chugging down what was left of my water.

"Because in short order Bernie's pretty head was laying on one of my pillows."

The water careened down the wrong pipe causing me to cough uncontrollably. Did my grandfather just admit to having an affair with a married woman?

There was a soft knock followed by Nurse Irma entering the room with a look of alarm on her face. "Are you OK sweetie?"

I waved my hand trying to indicate I was fine, still unable to fully articulate words.

Irma provided three firm taps to my back dislodging the water.

"Thanks," I managed to cough out.

"Time for bingo, Franklin."

Glancing at my watch, I rolled my eyes. I wasn't ready to end our visit, but trying to stop him from going to bingo would be a fool's task.

Grandpa rushed to the bathroom, and when I say rush I mean walked as briskly as a man of his age could. This conversation would have to wait until next week. Maybe this was for the best, it would allow me some time to do a little research and prepare a list of questions. Packing up my stuff, I gave Pops a quick hug, he'd put on cologne again. It was a fresh spritz he intentionally applied right before heading off to bingo. I was seventy-five percent certain Pops had a little lady friend he was entertaining. But I wasn't gonna pry as I was already elbow deep in his business as it was.

In the hall I saw August hanging out by the vending machines. When he caught sight of me his face lit up. Like legit lit up. It had been a while since a man's face became soft and carefree when he saw me.

"Hi." I tried not to return his goofy smile, but the corners of my mouth had a mind of their own.

"Hey ... do you wanna go get some coffee?"

"Yes." I barely allowed him to finish his sentence.

"Cool."

LAYING NEXT to one another in his bed I listened to his heavy breathing steadily return to its even, predictable pace. It was like August knew exactly what my body needed because he was craving the exact same thing. Escape. When our bodies were intertwined it was as if I was unburdened by all the things that weighed me down. It was just the two of us. I was still in space but it was more like a controlled fall, knowing I was tethered to something versus the endless descent into nothingness I usually experienced.

"Do you ever think about who your parents were before they had you?" I asked, angling my body toward him.

"What do you mean like what they did?"

"No more like who they were. What they dreamed about. Who they hoped to be before life intervened."

"Honestly, no. I've never really given it much thought."

"See, and that's the thing because one day you're gonna be the parent but you'll have had this whole life experience that shaped who you were before that. Like, to me, my mom is just my mom but she's so much more than that, she's Amy Jacobs. And I'm sure Amy dreamed of a life vastly different than the one she now has. My mom had me when she was fifteen."

"Damn."

"Yeah right. At fifteen I was smoking weed and letting guys feel me up. I was in no way capable of taking care of a newborn."

"I see some things never change. You're still letting guys feel you up." August joked.

"Very funny." I moved closer to him resting my chin on his chest. "What's your dream?"

August looked over at me, his face a puzzle. "I don't know."

"Bullshit." I climbed back on top of him straddling him with my knees on either side. "Everyone has a dream."

His eyes narrowed like he was deciding whether to trust me or not. "I wanna open up an auto shop, eventually having a chain of shops throughout the city."

"Wow, that's dope and entrepreneurial."

He smiled, encouraged by my response. "Yeah, I want it to have a real community vibe. A place people can trust and partner with. A place that uplifts and empowers our community." His smile faded. "I know it's just an auto repair shop but still."

"No, I think it sounds great. Being rooted in the neighborhood. Black owned. A spot that's reliable that's not gonna rip people off or upcharge because I'm a woman and they don't think I know any better."

"Yeah, exactly and rooted just like you said. I'm talking, hosting school supply drives and turkeys on Thanksgiving. Sponsoring the local basketball team or cheerleading squad. Shit we'll sponsor the debate club. I'm all about that black excellence."

As he talked, his hands absentmindedly rubbed my back, his hands and the confidence of his words were turning my core to molten lava. Grabbing his face, I plunged my tongue in his mouth. He responded just as I hoped, wrapping his massive arms around me, pushing my naked body against his.

I don't know what it was about this man's embrace that made me feel safe. Maybe because he was so big and it was almost like being wrapped in a fuzzy, warm blanket. August reminded me of a Sunday afternoon. The type of day when it's cold outside. You have a hot cup of tea, a good book and that comfy blanket to keep you warm. Maybe you'd fall asleep on the couch for an hour then wake up and have a snack. Yep, August was like Sundays, my favorite day of the week.

Releasing my hold on his lips, I scratched at his beard. "Tell me more."

"My buddy Sly and I just signed a lease on a shop. It needs to be cleaned up but we hope to open it in a few months. New coat of paint, a good scrub ..."

As August talked, I kissed my way down the length of his body, settling in between his legs. When I placed the tip of his penis in my warm mouth, he was rendered speechless.

WHEN I GOT to room three thirty, I was greeted by Nurse Irma.

"Hey Seraphina." Irma's face bore a strained expression.

"What's wrong? Is everything OK?" When you have a loved one in a place like this your first instinct was to assume the worst.

"Everything's fine. He's just been having a rough day is all."

"I wanna see him." I tried to brush past her but Irma caught me by the shoulders pushing me back. I shot her an icy glare and she immediately released her hold. I was taught to respect my elders but when it came to my family, I didn't play.

"Of course, you can see him, but maybe no stories today. We don't want to agitate him any further." Her tone reminded me of my father who questioned why I would want to dig up the past. I wasn't looking for trouble, I was looking to preserve our history. Too many families are losing their recipes. The secret ingredient that makes us who we are. We were casting aside the art of oral history as our lineage diminished. I want my family history rooted in facts, not watered down from being passed along like a game of telephone. Time was a thief, Pops was a prime example of that.

After Nurse Irma's admonishment, I opened the door to Pops' room. It was dimly lit, the curtains drawn. "Hey Pops it's me." I tried to keep my voice upbeat and cheery.

"I told you I don't want no damn Jell-O," he barked.

"No Jell-O just me ... Seraphina." I inched into the room slowly taking a seat in the chair across from him. "Nurse Irma said it's been a rough day."

"Nurse Irma? I don't know who that woman is, but she ain't no nurse. She ain't even got on those white stockings. If she's a nurse, I'm Nat King Cole."

"I know who that is." My face lit up. Sometimes he would reference people I'd have to Google later, but Nat King Cole I knew.

"What? ... What are you doing here? Meli I'm not going back and forth with you on this. I'm leaving. I don't want no cornbread, your cornbread ain't even sweet."

I watched helplessly as he had conversations with the past. Floating from one memory to the next. This wasn't the first time I'd seen him like this, but each time it cut me to the white meat. It started with him forgetting things and talking to himself, but when he threatened to beat my father's ass because he couldn't recall who he was, that's when my grandmother and father knew something was wrong and took him to see Dr. Crawford. Pops was diagnosed with early onset Alzheimer's four years ago.

I reached for his hand but he recoiled from my touch. "I don't know you. Don't you touch me."

"Grandpa, it's me." My voice pleaded hoping he'd remember, but his vacant expression told me he didn't.

"I'm a ranger in the Fifth Battalion. I don't know what you've been told." He burst into a military cadence reciting the song line for line.

How could he remember that but not me? My face grew warm as the tears I was trying to keep at bay broke free, streaming down my face. I cried in the dark room for several minutes, my arms clutching my chest as I swayed back and forth, while Pops talked about random points in time. A foot race with a boy from the neighborhood. Building a crib for his first born. And Bernie, he mentioned her name a lot.

Pops's dry hands found mine. "Shh child, dry your eyes. What's all the tears for?"

I clung to his hand, which was in desperate need of lotion. I could tell from his dark eyes he still didn't remember me, but he was attempting to console me and I needed that more than anything. I fell from my chair, planting my head on his knee. Like I had so many times in my youth. I'd rest my head on Pops knee and he'd tell me stories, make believe ones about brave girls who could do anything and conquer the world. It wasn't until I was in my teens that I realized the brave little girls in the stories Pops spun were me.

In Pops's mind I was smart and talented and bound for great things. When I moved to New York it seemed like he was right. But the rise was short and the crash back down to earth was bumpy. Pops's hand found my head and he patted it softly as I wept. I knew I should stop. I knew this was not helping him but the sadness that hovered over me like a dark cloud opened up, unleashing all my fears.

I didn't want to forget my grandfather but more importantly I didn't want him to forget me. He'd been good for several weeks and I'd secretly talked myself into believing he was getting better. Maybe the medication was actually working. But now it was clear, while the medicine may be slowing the clock, it was still ticking.

By the end of my visit, Pops focused all his attention out of the window preferring to pretend I wasn't there. Heading to the first floor, I spotted August posted up in his usual spot. He waved when he caught sight of me but I didn't stop, I just headed out the door. I needed fresh air and a safe place to cry as the second wave of tears hit me.

In my hot ass car, I rested my head on the steering wheel, my shoulders convulsing as the tears fell. Today was a mild day, it could be worse, sometimes he got violent. Other times he worked himself into a tizzy and he couldn't be consoled. You would just have to wait for him to tire himself out, oftentimes breaking things while cussing you out. Where was the pause button when you needed it? If this was what the future held, I didn't want any parts.

There was a soft tap on the driver's side window. I turned my head slightly to find August outside my car.

"Are you OK? Is it your grandpa?"

Nope, I wasn't interested in bearing my soul to my newfound fuck buddy. "I'm fine. It's fine." I yelled through the partially cracked window.

"You're clearly not fine, you're crying."

I stuck the key in the ignition and listened as the engine sputtered like my Uncle Mel, who coughed up a lung from his pack a day habit. I hated this car. It wasn't made for quick getaways or dramatic exits. One time I got into a huge fight with the dude I was seeing at the time and jumped in my little car only for it to stall on me. I had to turn around and ask if he would call AAA because my phone was dead. Yep, this car stayed embarrassing me.

Finally, Dorothy Zbornak turned over. My little Toyota was cranky but she always got the job done, much like Dorothy from the Golden Girls. I slowly pulled off, not looking at August who was standing outside my car, probably questioning his choice in women.

I didn't want to talk about what was happening with Pops. Words held power and speaking about the shift in the man I knew, and the fact that I was perpetually in a state of grief even when I hadn't even lost him yet, was not something I wanted to release into the universe. So I would do what I always did ... pretend. Pretend everything was fine, pretend I was happy, pretend I had it all together.

AUGUST

"RED NISSAN SENTRA," I called out to the half-full waiting room.

"That's me." A woman jumped up, her arm full of bangles making music on her wrist with each step.

"You look familiar," I said when she stopped at the counter.

"Really, where you know me from?" She batted her eyes at me, breaking my stone facade.

Tilting my head, my memories clicked into place. This was the woman who ditched Seraphina at the bar a few weeks back. Which was a dick move, but one I was grateful she'd made. "Aren't you Seraphina's friend?"

She narrowed her eyes examining my face. "I'm her cousin. How do you know Sera?"

Sera? I liked it, hopefully Seraphina and I got close enough and I'd be able to also call her by that nickname.

"We met at the Red Cup a few weeks ago." I opted to omit our true first meeting, at the nursing home.

She snapped her long fingers and said, "I remember you. I'm Junie by the way."

"August." Grabbing a clipboard, I walked from behind the

counter. "Let's head to your car so I can show you what I found."

Lifting the hood, I ran down the list of things needing to be addressed.

"All that sounds like a lot of money." Junie stared at her vehicle with disdain.

"You missed three scheduled maintenance appointments. And your car is well over a hundred-thousand miles. Nissans are reliable but they're not work horses."

"You sound like my father."

"Sounds like he's a smart guy." I could tell from her face I was losing her and she was two seconds away from dropping the hood and driving this car away. "Look, we don't have to do everything now. But there are things that have to get done today if you want this car to continue to run."

"What are those things and how much are we talking?"

"Oil change. Your oil reservoir is dryer than that brick wall over there and spark plugs. They're shot and that's why you're having issues with the car starting."

Junie poked out her lips considering my recommendations.

"If you don't spend the one fifty today, you'll be paying five hundred tomorrow to get that shit towed."

"OK, oil change and spark plugs. I ain't paying for shit else."

As we walked back to the shop I decided to crawl out on a limb.

"How's Seraphina?"

"Good."

"Weird question. Could you give me her number? I wanted to ask her something?"

"You two ain't exchange numbers?"

"We hadn't gotten to that part yet, exactly."

"Well, if Sera didn't give you her number I'm not about to do it. That's creepy."

She was right, my request was kinda on the stalker level. But I just wanted to make sure she was good. She was really upset this past Sunday and if there was something I could do to make her feel better, then I wanted to offer my assistance. And no this was not because I was looking to hook up again. Of course, I wanted that but I also wanted her to be OK.

I stopped at the shop door. "Normally I wouldn't ask this but I saw her on Sunday and she seemed pretty upset and I just wanted to check on her."

"Sunday?"

"Yeah, at Summercrest, it's an old folks' home."

"I know that it is. What was she upset about?"

"I don't know, but she was crying so I was concerned." I hoped I wasn't saying too much. I didn't know how close Seraphina was to her cousin and the last thing I wanted to do was overstep.

Junie worked her lips into a pucker. "If I were to give you her information what's in it for me?"

I hoisted an uneasy shoulder not following where she was heading.

Junie hissed out an annoyed sigh. "How much you taking off that one fifty?"

"Wait, so you're bartering with your cousin's personal info?"

"We both have something the other wants. I want my car fixed on the cheap and you wanna get into Seraphina's pants."

"I do not wanna get ... you know what, never mind. Could you just check on her and make sure she's OK." I wasn't opposed to giving out discounts but it seemed a bit fiendish to obtain her number in this way. Holding the door, we reentered the shop.

After completing the maintenance, I called Junie to the register for payment. "Ok, we changed the oil, rotated the tires and switched out the spark plugs. I also drained and added new coolant fluid at no additional charge. Your total is one hundred and seventy dollars after taxes."

Junie whipped out a credit card she had to swipe three times before it was accepted.

"Thank you for trusting your car to Arturo's Auto Rider and remember Art has you covered." I handed Junie her keys.

Junie pulled a pen out of the coffee cup shaped like a stack of tires. "Don't make me regret this." She scribbled an address and number on the car evaluation form attached to my clipboard, before scooping up her keys and heading for the door.

Turning the clipboard, I noted the address. It was five minutes away from here. Ripping the sheet from the clipboard, I folded it and tucked it into the back pocket of my Dickies.

After work I went home for a quick shower and then jumped into my car and headed to the address Junie had provided. I don't know if this was a good idea or a bad one but I was committed, having parked a few houses down from Seraphina's spot. Should I have called before showing up at her door step, probably. But I didn't want to run the risk of her telling me she didn't want to see me. Climbing out of my Nova, I stopped in front of her house only now realizing I hadn't thought this all the way through.

What exactly was I gonna say when she answered the door? What if she was pissed that I just showed up unannounced? If the roles were reversed how would I feel? Honestly, if Seraphina and her thick thighs showed up unexpected at my door, I would gladly welcome it and would spend the remainder of the day showing her how much I appreciated her thoughtful consideration. I doubt her response would be similar.

With a deep breath I bounded up the steps, ringing the bell before I lost my nerve. Someone stirred inside, soft steps padded toward the front door. There was a long pause before the door swung open.

"Can I help you?"

"Uh, yes. Hello ma'am I'm looking for Seraphina." I sounded like a bumbling idiot.

"Seraphina?" Her eyebrow raised in disbelief.

"Yes ma'am."

"One second." She closed the door in my face. Locking it behind her. "Sera, honey someone is here to see you."

My chest tightened hearing the woman call her name. For a brief moment I thought maybe Junie gave me the wrong address. Why didn't I give this more consideration? What if she opened the door and asked what the fuck I was doing at her place? What if she turned on the sprinklers or called the cops? I'd blame it all on Junie.

The door opened and on the other side was Seraphina, wide eyed, her thick hair circling her face. She was dressed casually; I'd probably interrupted her reading a book or completing a crossword puzzle. She struck me as the type of woman that did things to stimulate her brain in her down time. Seraphina looked behind her at the woman who was lingering by the stairs trying to figure out who I was and why I was here.

"It's OK Mom, I know him." Seraphina moved over the threshold closing the door behind her. "What are you doing here?"

"I wanted to check in on you."

"So you what, stalked me online and found my address?"

"No, because that would be weird."

"This *is* weird."

"Junie gave me your address." I blurted out hoping that would make my unexpected visit better.

"Again, what are you doing here?"

"I was worried about you. You seemed upset the last time I saw you and—"

"I'm fine." She was stone still but she was casting sidelong glances in my direction.

"I don't usually cry when I'm fine."

"You need to learn to mind your business." She crossed her arms over her chest.

"I was just trying to be a friend. I didn't mean to overstep." My feet were already retreating from the porch. This was a mistake.

The front door opened wide. "Do you and your friend want something to drink? It's hot out there." Seraphina's mother asked, her eyes wide with curiosity as they moved from her daughter to me.

"No, thanks ma'am I was just leaving."

Seraphina dropped her arms from her chest. "You don't have to go. I mean if you want you could stay for a bit. If you want."

I placed my feet back on the top of the porch. "I would like that." I smiled down at Seraphina whose demeanor was hard to read. I couldn't tell if she was annoyed or happy that I had agreed to stay.

"Great," Seraphina's mother exclaimed. "I just made some sun brewed tea."

Sitting in the sunny living room, I took a sip of the ice-cold tea, that was just the right amount of sweet. "This is delicious, thank you."

"So how do you know Seraphina?"

"We met at Summercrest." Seraphina answered for me.

Mrs. Jacobs's eyes grew wide. "I knew there had to be more going on over there than just visiting your grandfather."

Seraphina gave her mother a roll of her big, brown eyes.

"Mother please, it's not like that. August and I are just … friends."

Friends? You know what I'll take it. I'd rather be considered a friend than some random booty call. Friend I could work with. The distance from friend to boyfriend wasn't that big a leap.

"Sorry," Mrs. Jacobs said in an exaggerated tone. "I wasn't trying to start anything. Just happy to see you hanging out with some new people. I worry the friends you associate with are bad influences."

I could understand that, Junie seemed like a bad egg.

"Mother I'm thirty-three I can't be influenced."

"Well, you've made some not-so-great choices recently so—"

"And all of those choices I made completely on my own. So if you're looking for someone to blame you can blame me."

"I'm not looking to lay blame." Her mother flashed a pleasant smile in my direction. It was clear she was uncomfortable with the trajectory of this conversation.

"Do you think you could give August and me a minute alone?" Seraphina asked her mother.

"Of course, sweetie. Sure. If you two need anything just holler."

When her mother was out of ear shot Seraphina said, "She is always hovering."

"I'm sure she's just worried about you."

"I'm fine. So there is no need for anyone to worry." She made her best attempt to smile bright but her face looked more like a caricature of a happy person. "I'm sorry you came over here for nothing."

"Well, I got to see you, so that makes it worth it."

Seraphina narrowed her warm, brandy-brown eyes. I knew that look when a woman was trying to figure out if I was full of shit or not. This particular woman seemed cautious when it came to letting others in. I could only assume it was associated with some hurt or disappointment from her past. I hoped she could see I wasn't looking to add to that hurt.

"Hey, do you wanna get out of here? We could go grab some din—"

"Yes." She interrupted before I could finish my sentence. "Give me fifteen minutes?"

"I'll be right here."

She jumped up from the couch. Before heading for the stairs, she turned and said, "You are not obligated to answer any of my mother's nosy questions."

eleven

THE LAST TIME I was out with a guy on a work night … damn it's been a long time. Most of my nights were spent locked in my bedroom or watching reruns with my parents. Pathetic, I know. The highlight of my day most nights was correctly guessing the daily double. So being out with August was a nice change of pace. In the fifteen minutes I'd had to get ready, I changed into a striped sundress and switched my underwear to a lacey, matching pair. Lastly, I refreshed my hair, letting my natural twists and coils fall effortlessly, brushing my shoulder.

When I opened the door and found him on the other side, I was pissed but he seemed genuinely concerned for me. How do you cuss someone out for caring? And it was nice to have a distraction from all the craptastic events in my life. That's what this was, a distraction. I wasn't looking to get attached right now. Relationships required work and I was in the middle of actively trying to fix my life. Adding a new player to this already difficult level of adulting was not a part of the plan.

August took us to a BBQ joint with brown paper towels and sauce in squeeze bottles. When our food came the amount of the serving could probably feed four other people. But August made easy work of his plate. I guess when you weigh close to two hundred and fifty pounds a family-feast-sized plate was light work.

"I can see why this is your favorite place." I licked sweet and spicy BBQ sauce from my fingers.

"It's good right?" The corners of his mouth curled upward. "Next time you'll have to take me to your favorite spot."

"Next time? That's very presumptuous."

"What, I don't get a next time?"

"Honestly, I'm just trying to make it through this day. I'm not really focused on the next."

August sniffed at my response, taking a drink from his beer bottle. "And Sunday?"

"You're not gonna let that go, are you?"

"If you want me to, I will. But I just want you to know if you need to talk, or vent, or scream, or cry you can do that with me."

"You don't even know me." My face tightened as my brows drew closer.

"I'm trying really hard to change that."

I'd never been good at opening up. I was great at getting others to share their stories while never being willing to do the same. I learned early on that everyone had something going on. Their own struggles and fears and I had no right to burden them with my own. So I opted to hold it all inside. I was like an old stick of dynamite, while I looked fine from the outside, inside I was unstable and could pop off at any moment.

"Don't ask for things that you'll end up regretting." I wagged a finger of warning in his direction.

"Getting to know you? I doubt I'd ever regret that."

"You have your own shit; you don't need mine too."

August pushed our plates aside, reaching for my hands. The fact that I didn't instinctually pull away was a good sign. I needed to be touched. Craved it actually. And this simple gesture, his fingers interlocked with mine, was shiver inducing.

"I'm terrified that my mother is gonna die in that home. Family's important to me and I know it would be hard caring for her on my own, but she took care of me for years, now it's my turn to return the favor." He rolled his broad shoulders. "I don't even know what that looks like but I'm willing to sacrifice if that means my mother can live the final years of her life with dignity."

I squeezed his hand, his eyes were determined but I could still recognize the fear that lay underneath. "I'm sorry." I wished I could offer more than that empty sentiment.

He shook my words off. "Your turn."

August was sitting across from me giving me what I needed; a listening ear. He had no idea the Pandora's box he was attempting to open. I was a closed book until I wasn't. When I trusted someone, I told them everything, from the random thoughts that pinged around my brain to my deepest, darkest and oftentimes, irrational fears. There was something about this gentle bear of a man that made me want to trust him. I mean he'd gone through a lot to get to this point.

Getting my address from Junie must have involved some serious sweet talk with the promise of a returned favor, which Junie would hold him to like a pesky bill collector. Then having the balls to show up to my place and knock on the door not knowing what mood he'd find me in. Studying his face filled with earnest anticipation, I decided to throw him a bone.

"My grandfather has Alzheimer's. Some days he's great but then there are others when he doesn't remember. Sunday was one of those days. He didn't remember me and it broke my heart." I dissolved into tears sobbing loudly, surprising myself. Just when I thought I was all cried out I would find a new bottomless well to pull from.

August stood, sliding into the booth next to me. His massive arms wrapped around me pulling me close. Burying my face in his solid chest, I babbled incoherently. "I know I've had years to come to terms with this but it hasn't gotten any easier. Junie tells me I'm being a baby about the whole thing and it's just the circle of life. I don't wanna hear that shit, this is my grandfather, not *The Lion King*. I don't want him dying alone without the memory of the people who love him to provide some comfort." I inched back looking up at his face. "So that's why I was crying on Sunday. I know it's stupid, but—"

"It's not stupid. You love your grandfather, ain't no shame in that."

"Most visits he's great, even remembering things I've long forgotten." I sniffled, using the scratchy, brown paper towel to dry my tears.

"I'm sure seeing you helps. Keeps him from feeling like an afterthought."

"That's what I tell my dad. He hasn't visited Pops in months. I think he feels guilty about sticking him in that place. And Pops is still pissed about it. The last time my father came with me for a visit, they got into a yelling match. Pops got all worked up. And now my dad thinks it's best to just stay away."

"I can understand that. It took me three months before I finally made the trip to see my mom at Summercrest. I just felt guilty. Guilty for not being there, for not fighting harder. And as the weeks ticked past, I felt guilty because I hadn't made the trip." August leaned back in the booth. "I'm trying hard to fix that now. I want my mom to know she's not forgotten, or a burden. Even if all we do is play cards or I help her with one of her puzzles, at least I'm there."

"That's why I visit Pops every week. We talk about his life. I get to memorialize it but I secretly hope that reliving his past will make it harder to forget."

"I get it, Summercrest is like a graveyard; it's where old people go to die. I'll be damned if my mom is just hidden away in some room waiting out the clock. She deserves better and so does your grandfather. When my dad died last year it was rough on all of us but especially her, she hadn't been alone in over sixty years."

"Damn, that's crazy ... sixty years. People don't love like that anymore." I eased out of his arms feeling silly for my crying fit.

"No, they don't. Everything has become disposable, even love."

"We have more options now. Marriage and kids aren't the end game for many people anymore. My grandpa was married four times to three different women. He wasn't very good at love but he was always willing to try."

"And you?"

"Me?"

"How's that love thing working out for you?"

The last guy I loved ended up cheating on me with my best friend so if I was being completely honest, love was kicking my ass. "I'm still trying to figure it out." I dropped my eyes, embarrassed by the gaze of his intense, brown eyes. "I bet your mother has some great stories to tell you about her and your father. Things you probably never knew or thought to ask. There are amazing stories to be found in the elders in our families and right in our community." I downed the rest of my Arnold Palmer. "You know Mr. Hammond, who collects cans in the neighborhood?"

"You mean the old dude with the busted wagon?"

"Yes."

"Yeah. I thought he was crazy."

"He's not. He used to be a jazz musician playing with some of the greats. They called him Sweetback because of the sounds he made on his saxophone."

"How'd you find all that out?"

"I talked to him. He was a big deal when I was growing up. He didn't always have that wagon, for a long time he had a Cadillac with the cleanest, green-candy-apple paint."

August pulled his face. "Hmm, I wouldn't have thought it."

"Yeah, that's the thing about people. Oftentimes we just see who a person is in this moment and not who they were or wanted to be. Like you see me, a woman in her thirties living with her parents, it's pretty pathetic."

"That's not how I see you." His eyes narrowed as he reached to brush a stray twist of hair from my face.

"Oh yeah, how do you see me?" My stomach tightened into knotted coils as I braced myself for his answer.

"You're the woman that finds beauty in places that others could not no matter how hard they looked. You're inquisitive, and you have an easy way about you that makes people wanna open up. I don't know if it's because they see the sadness and hurt in your eyes and that makes them comfortable enough to reveal long held secrets, because they know your questions aren't followed up by judgment."

"Sadness and hurt?" I squinted up at him.

"Don't get me wrong, I also see this fierce desire in your eyes for something more."

"Go on."

"I see a woman who doesn't smile often but when she does it's like high beams it's so bright, drawing everyone's attention. You're curious, your brain is always three steps ahead. You're sexy as hell without even trying. And you are clearly smarter than me and I love that shit."

Warmth whooshed up my neck crossing over my cheeks. "See now you're just trying to get into my pants."

"I wasn't, I swear." He held up his three middle fingers. "But if that's something you want, I'm more than willing to provide it."

We both knew I wanted it. We both knew I would let him do almost anything to me if it ended like our last few encounters, which left my entire body vibrating as the endorphins and oxytocin flooded my insides, making me feel completely at peace. When he was inside me the only thing I could think about was how good he felt, the innate smell of him driving me insane.

"It's late, we should go." It was only nine o'clock, but the things I wanted to do to August were much better suited for behind closed doors.

twelve

IN THE CAR I decided to take the long way home. With the windows down, the soft, warm breeze caused the ruffled sleeves of Seraphina's dress to flutter as if dancing to the hum of the night. I knew that Seraphina and I weren't operating under titles. What was happening between us wasn't thought out or planned. Just two people enjoying one another's energy. But being with her was effortless.

I didn't have to try to impress her. For starters, she wasn't a woman who was easily impressed. But more importantly, she seemed genuinely content with who I was. She wasn't looking to upgrade me or round my rough edges. I got the distinct impression she liked the sharp edges and the potential pain they could inflict.

I was pretty sure she didn't see this as a date. Maybe I was a means to an end. She was hanging out with me ... so she could benefit from my dick hitting her spot, making her holler. Reaching for her hand I whispered a silent prayer that she didn't retreat from my touch or make a joke to dampen the mood. She looked at me with curiosity in her eyes but she didn't let my hand go. Rubbing my thumb over her soft skin, I had trouble wiping away the goofy smile tugging at the corners of my mouth.

Back at my humble abode, I placed the car in park. I hadn't even asked her if she wanted to spend the night, which now felt like a miscalculation. "I can take you home if you want. I'm not expecting, we don't have to … Shit, we could just chill and watch Family Guy reruns if you want."

Seraphina leaned in, pressing her soft lips against mine, ending my blathering. Scooping my arm around her, I pulled her over the center console that divided us until she was straddling my lap. Plunging my hands into her fluffy hair, I pulled her close. Our kisses were wild and rabid.

I honestly couldn't get enough of this woman. The soft sounds she made while my mouth explored hers caused my face to flush. Seraphina's fingernails scratched at my beard as her hips floated over my lap. She bit my bottom lip and I returned the favor, giving her thick thighs a smack. I eased my hand down her lacy boy-short underwear, running a finger down her crack before grabbing hold.

Seraphina's lips slipped from mine as she planted kisses on my face and neck. Her lips landed on the base of my ear causing my body to tense, tightening my hold around her ass. "I really like you." I breathed out.

She stopped kissing me looking down at my face. Had I said something wrong? Taken this casual hook up too far?

"I like you too." She rubbed her thumb over my mouth.

"Fair warning, I'm getting attached. So if this ain't what you want maybe we should press pause right now."

"I don't know what I want. But I'm willing to let this play through."

OK, you heard that too right. She just said that she liked me and she wanted to get dicked down by me consistently and if I introduced her to people as my girlfriend, she was cool with that. Because that is definitely what I heard.

"I have a feeling this is gonna be a very long movie, the kind with multiple after credit scenes."

"I hope you don't end up disappointed." She dropped her eyes, pressing her forehead against mine.

"With you? Impossible." I whispered over her mouth. I was gonna love the fuck out of this woman, she'd never wanna let me go.

We weren't even completely over the threshold of my place before I was pulling Seraphina's underwear over her thick thighs. Grabbing hold of her I hoisted her upward hooking her legs over my shoulders bringing her sweet spot level with my face. Seraphina gasped from the precarious position bracing her hand against the door. Flexing my tongue, I performed tiny circles over her clit. I buried my face in between her folds not wanting to miss a single spot.

Seraphina's quavering legs made balancing her difficult, but one advantage to being this big was my raw strength. Grabbing her ass, I hoped she felt confident that I had her with no intentions of letting her fall. When Seraphina screamed out my name it sent me into a trance like state my only focus pleasing her. Her sweet juices ran down my chin and my dick pressed against my pants ready to tag in.

She writhed her hip over my tongue her body practically folding over as she shivered six feet off the ground. I helped her dismount and when her feet touched the floor her legs wobbled. A sign of a job well done. But I wasn't done, directing her to the couch I removed her dress before falling out of my own clothes. Rolling a condom over my dick I bent her over the back of the couch entering her from behind.

Seraphina's breathing hitched in that predictable way it always did when I first slide inside. I started with slow effortless strokes building in intensity in conjunction with her prompting. Slipping my hand between her legs I massaging her clit while continuing to thrust from behind. Seraphina released a full throated scream making me thankful I lived in a detached garage and not an apartment with shared walls.

Backing away I turned her around sliding back in I lifted her up and standing in the middle of my place I guided her up and down my stiff dick while she begged me for more. Seraphina's words all the motivation I needed to maintain my potent pace. Her perky breast spun in small circles with each slide down my shaft. Dropping her to the bed I snuck in some much-needed kisses while my fingers worked themselves deep into her core. Seraphina's lips trembled against mine as her second orgasm of the night washed over her.

Sliding back inside it wasn't long before her speech became incoherent. Her nails scraping down my back. She whimpered her body convulsing. The sight of her unfiltered desire for me twinkling in her eyes assisted my release. Plunging my face into her neck I groaned as her walls tighten around me. God I'd hit the jackpot with this woman.

I planted soft kisses on her cheek and collarbone.

"It appears dating August Gardner comes with tons of perps," she cooed.

"You ain't seen nothing yet," I said devouring her lips.

thirteen

SERAPHINA

"SO, TELL ME MORE ABOUT BERNIE." It was Sunday and once again I'd made the thirty-minute drive to Summercrest to visit Pops. I'd called ahead to check on his disposition and was told that he was having a good day. Truthfully, if they said anything different, I don't think I would've made the trip. Seeing Pops was always the highlight of my week. But last weekend was tough and kind of wrecked me.

Maybe it was selfish of me to expect him to be who he was when I was a ten-year-old girl who thought her Pops could walk on water. We'd both changed. I wasn't as naive, or easily impressed, and the spark of hope I once had that anything was possible for me had long faded. I knew now that life was hard and even if you did everything right, shit could still go terribly wrong.

Pops rubbed the whiskers on his face. "What do you know so far?"

"You said she was the love of your life, but when you went off to war she ended up marrying someone else." I could only imagine how painful that must have been for him. I'd recently learned that my ex-boyfriend, Todd, had gotten engaged to the same *friend* I'd caught him cheating on me with. That news stung like a son of a bitch and Todd was in no way the love of my life, so I'm sure Pops was pretty torn up when Bernie moved on.

"Yes, that's right. When I got back to Detroit she was married and had a newborn. I was married too, having eventually moved on marrying the second prettiest girl in my high school senior class."

My face lit up. "Grandma Maye." Maye was Pops's first wife. She wasn't my grandmother but she treated me like family nonetheless. Even though her and Pops didn't work out, she was still at every family function bumping heads with Grandma Loretta. Those two women couldn't stand one another, maybe because they were so similar.

"Yep," Pops released a rueful laugh. "That woman was a chatterbox, she never shut up. When I was with her, I knew everybody's business because she was more informative than the six o'clock news. She knew all the neighborhood secrets."

"I know there has to be more to you and Bernie. When did you two reconnect?" I directed the conversation back to Bernie because if I let him, he'd tell me some obscure story that was completely unrelated.

"Shortly after I returned to the States."

My eyebrows raised slightly but I didn't say a word. I knew that Pops was a playboy, I mean a man like him doesn't get married four times without a little relationship overlap. Pops noticed me internally clutching my pearls.

"Not my finest moment, I'll admit that. But Bernie and I were hooked."

Love is funny that way it knows no bounds. It can't be contained by time or distance it just continues to exist in perpetual longing.

Pops continued, "Even though we'd both moved on and

Bernadette was a mother and I had a baby on the way I couldn't let her go."

I jotted her name down in my notepad, Bernadette, drawing a line under it. When I got home, I planned on Googling that name to see if any local matches popped up. "You two started seeing one another again?"

He nodded his head slowly. "We'd sneak off … go for long drives, or meet up at the library. When you say you're heading to the library people tend to assume you're looking for a new book not playing kissy face behind the building."

"So you and Bernadette had an affair?"

Pops waved his hand between us pushing my words away. "I don't like that word."

"OK, what would you like to call it?"

He turned his attention to the window thinking for a moment. I sat in silence just letting his mind work. The secret to journalism was to get people talking. Most people just wanted to be heard to get their personal truth out. And the times that I'd allowed them to do that unfettered often made for the most insightful interviews. Listening was a skill and I was great at it, mostly because I hated talking about myself.

"It was an adventure." Pop's deep raspy voice finally broke the silence. "Every minute with her was more thrilling than the next. Now I don't want you thinking it was all physical because it was so much more than that. She was so much more than that." Pops turned to face me once again. "You ever meet someone who just turns your gray days blue?

"It didn't matter that my boss talked to me like I was a child even though I was the most qualified man on that team. Didn't matter that I only had ten dollars in my pocket and payday was a week and a half away. It didn't matter that the baby Maye was carrying was born still and she was inconsolable and I felt useless. Bernadette was able to make all the real-world shit disappear even if only for a little while."

"How'd she do that?"

Pops hitched his shoulders while rubbing his knees with his hands. "It was in her laugh and the way she would float across a room, her hair pinned high showing off her long delicate neck. The way she'd reach for me and pull me close. She smelt like jasmine, sweet and light and I loved to bury my face in her—"

"TMI Pops." I warned wagging a finger at him.

"I was gonna say her hair." He let out a rascally laugh. "That woman made me feel like a man in a world that seemed intent on tearing me down and putting me in my place." He got that far off look that people got when they were reminiscing. "I got it from every angle, couldn't even be easy in my own home. Maye was disappointed in me because I couldn't be the man she wanted me to be. It's a hard pill to swallow having to live with someone who's tired of loving you. I loved Maye, just not in the way she needed.

"Then there was the job where people looked past me to ask the white boy what he thought, even though I was a gotdamn engineer. I'm a man who likes to speak plainly but at Fleet Tech I had to bite my tongue and take crap no one should have to." Pops shook his head. "But with Bernie all that meant nothing cause when I looked into her round brown eyes, I could see she believed in me. And it made me wanna work hard and prove all the naysayers wrong."

A shiver tripped up my spine at the realization that August had that same effect on me. The way he would look at me with excitement and anticipation for my next word, like I was a poet laureate or something. Or how his hand found mine in the car and my body relaxed into the leather seat as he rubbed his thumb over the base of my fingers. In that moment nothing else mattered but he and I and the sound of D'Angelo floating from the speakers. It was in the way his arms pulled me close and held me through the night, never letting go. So that in the morning I was nestled in a cocoon of his massive wingspan.

No. August wasn't the love of my life, that would be stupid, I've known him for all of a month and a half. That would be silly, right? But I did know that the bad stuff didn't seem so scary when I was with him. Shaking the thought from my head I asked, "How long did you and Ms. Bernadette go on these adventures?"

"Oh, off and on for years. At different points we vowed to stop. She'd end things with me. And believe it or not a few times I ended it with her. Like when I met Loretta. But eventually like moths to a flame we found each other. Not like we had to look far since for much of that time we lived on the same block."

"Hold up, you lived on the same block?" I leaned forward having difficulty believing what I was hearing.

"Yep, our kids would play together."

This affair sounded messy. *How do you pretend to be just neighbors when you know it was so much more?*

"Did you ever get caught?"

"Why do you think your grandmother left me?"

I'd never given much thought to why he and my grandmother split. But cheating would definitely do it. "How come you and Bernadette never tried to make a real go at a relationship?"

"She was married. And she had them girls. They were like stair steps one right after the other."

I was tempted to ask if any of her kids were his but thought better of it.

Pops continued, "They were too little to be ripped away from their father. Bernie didn't have her father growing up and she wanted better for them girls. I would've run away with her in a heartbeat but she was committed to her family." Pops ran his long boney finger over his mouth. "There was one time I thought she was ready to leave Auggie and we were talking real serious. Her girls were getting older … but she was afraid he'd fight for full custody of the girls and win. That gave her pause, it made things harder."

It wasn't lost on me that in all of this not once did Pops mention his obligation to his own children. I knew from speaking with my dad that Pops wasn't the ideal father. He wasn't always around, often in the pool hall or race track. Grandma Loretta handled most of the raising, teaching, and discipline of my father and Uncle Chuck. Maybe I had Pops to thank for my dad being such a rigid disciplinarian, trying to make up for what was lacking in his childhood.

"What happened to Ms. Bernadette?"

"What time is it?" Pops scanned the room like he'd awaken from a dream and was unsure of how he'd gotten here.

"We still have a half hour before bingo."

"I can't be late."

"Understood. Where is Bernadette now?"

"She's with me. Close to me. Time split us apart but it's also brought us back together in this of all places."

"You mean she's always in your heart?"

"I'm saving her a seat at bingo." With those final words Pops stood slowly making his way to the bathroom to tidy up.

Pops dictated when the interviews were over. The fact that he was in the bathroom whistling an unfamiliar tune was my cue to pack it up. Stopping the recording feature on my phone, I loaded my notebook and pen into my backpack and returned both chairs to their respective spots in his room. Pops exited the bathroom smelling good with a wide smile on his face.

Reaching for his cane he said, "Walk me down."

I hooked my arm in his and we made the slow trek to the first-floor rec room. Pops maneuvered through the room, stopping to say hello to friends along the way before taking a seat and laying his cane on the seat next to his.

Turning to leave, I walked directly into a brick wall of a man.

"Whoa," August laughed, reaching for my arm so I didn't tumble to the floor.

"Augustine, you have to be more careful, you almost knocked this young lady to the ground." The woman, who I could only assume was his mother, said.

The corners of my mouth curled upward. *Augustine?*

He flashed me a warning letting me know that that name was off limits.

"Luckily, I know her. So hopefully there's no hard feelings?"

"No, actually I should have been paying attention to where I was going." I smiled.

August's mother looked from him to me. "So are you going to introduce me or have you forgotten your manners today too."

August chuckled at the ribbing from his mother. "Ah, Mom, this is my ... friend Seraphina."

When he called me his friend my heart jumped. I liked that he counted me as one of his friends.

"It's nice to meet you Mrs. Gardner. August failed to tell me how stylish his mother was."

Mrs. Gardner flashed a warm smile. In her crisp, white top and camel-colored shawl, she was quite the beauty. Beauty like hers was undeniable in spite of the gray hairs and subtle wrinkles that lined her face.

She pointed her perfectly manicured, red finger at me. "Oh, I like her."

The loud speaker squealed followed by a serene voice. "Bingo blitz night is starting in five minutes."

"Well, I must find my seat. It was nice meeting you dear." She tugged on August's sleeve and he lowered himself to her level so that she could plant a kiss on his cheek. I could hear her whisper in his ear. "She's prettier than you said." Giving me one last smile she entered the rec room.

"You look just like her, Augustine."

"Don't you even. Augustine is my father's name."

"So I can't call you that?"

"It depends on when and why you're saying it." He flashed a naughty grin. "Do you wanna hang out? We could go watch that new scary movie everyone's been talking about."

"If we go see that movie you'll have to hold me close."

"I can do that." His fingers found the swath of exposed skin along my waist.

I turned back to the rec room and spotted Mrs. Gardner settling in next to Pops. The smile on his face was a mile wide. I couldn't remember the last time I'd seen him smile like that. "Your mother's sitting next to my grandfather."

"She mentioned she had a friend here. Small world." August scooped my hand in his leading me toward the exit.

"Ah ... it's nice that they found one another." As the words left my mouth I stopped in my tracks looking back at Pops and August's mother sharing a laugh. His words from our forty-five-minute visit rolling over in my head. SHUT THE FRONT DOOR!

AUGUST

WHEN MY PHONE chimed on the nightstand, Seraphina grumbled from the crook between my neck which she now claimed as home. "Who sets an alarm on Saturday?" Her breath tickled my skin.

"I told you I have to meet Sly at the shop. If we want to open in two months we have to pick up the pace."

Seraphina released a soft moan. "Do you need help?" I could tell from her tone that this was a courtesy offer and she in no way intended on helping out.

"No, I got it."

"I'm really good at painting walls and shellacking, whatever that means." She planted a soft kiss to my neck.

"Maybe some other time." I didn't want her seeing the shop until it was ready. The last thing I needed was for her to walk into the shop with stains on the carpet and a huge hole in the wall and start second guessing why she was fucking with me.

"What do you have planned today?" I asked, playing with the soft curls that poked out of her headscarf.

"I'm braiding Junie's hair at noon." She lifted herself from the bed, shuffling to the bathroom.

This couple thing was working out nicely with Seraphina sleeping over most nights. I encouraged her to leave a toothbrush and other toiletries at my place, but without fail she made sure everything was neatly packed in her overnight bag before leaving.

"Will I see you later?" I hoped my question came off as casual.

"If you want to see me. I'm up to being seen," she said, reentering the room.

Reaching for her, I pulled her back to the bed so she was straddling me. "I always wanna see you."

"You're not bored of me yet?" she teased.

"How could I get bored with all of this?" I gave her ass a playful slap.

Her plump lips curved into a smile before meeting mine. Seraphina cupped my face, our tongues tickling, dancing, and sucking the other's. Sliding my hands to her ass, I worked her hips over my shaft. Her slickness making my dick come alive.

"You're gonna be late," she warned.

"Well then we better make it worth it." I groaned as I slid inside.

AT THE SHOP, Sly was trying to convince me that the split-pea-color paint he'd purchased was in fact the sea-salt green we'd agreed on.

"This is what you asked for, bro," Sly said.

"It looks like someone threw up in a paint can and you bought it."

"You wanted green and you got green. What can I tell you? We should have gone with red like I suggested."

"Red is not a soothing color. The waiting area needs to be a neutral color so that people feel relaxed and calm and don't get agitated if a repair takes longer than usual."

"OK Joanna Gaines, when did you become an interior designer?"

"Who the hell is Joanna Gaines?"

"HGTV," Sly said, shaking his head like this was common knowledge.

"I've had a long time to think about this and every detail counts. Just because we fix cars doesn't mean we slap some hubcaps on the wall and call it a day."

"Sounds like a lot of work. We have less than two months, you know?"

Looking around the empty space, I could see my vision as clear as day. "Seating will be over there." I pointed. "Over in the hall we'll have vending machines just in case customers get hungry." Spinning around I pointed to a corner near the service counter. "This is the perfect spot for the Keurig station, with a variety of coffee, tea, and hot chocolate for the kids."

Sly nodded thoughtfully and I could see his eyes come to life as I described each new detail. Gus and Sly's Auto Repair Shop was going to offer quality service and an exceptional customer experience.

"Well damn, we can't have all that with this ugly ass puke-tinged color on the wall. I'll head back to Home Depot and return it," Sly said.

"That's what I'm talking about. While you're doing that I'll patch up this wall." With Sly gone, I texted Seraphina.

Me: Did you make it home OK?

Seraphina: Yeah, sorry about that. I forgot to text you.

Me: It's cool. It's not like I worry about you or anything like that.

Seraphina: I'll get better. I promise.

Me: Alright, tell Junie I said hello.

Seraphina: Will do. Call me when you're done.

Me: First thing.

Seraphina: Oh shit, we've entered the heart emoji stage of this relationship?

Yes, that was a heart emoji. Yes, it was corny. But Seraphina made me want to send heart emojis and wear matching T-shirts. Mine would read "She's My Sweet Potato" and Seraphina's would read "I Yam." And people would laugh as we walked past but I wouldn't even care because this woman is amazing and the sex is slap your momma good.

Me: Is this better?

Seraphina:

I laughed at my phone screen. This was all new but I had a good feeling about us. Truth be told, I think I was ready to do more than just send heart emojis. I'd been seriously considering asking Seraphina to move in. Sure, my place was the size of ... well a two-car garage but bumping into her every morning would be the nicest way to start my day. But first I needed to get this shop open. Once I did I'd be in a better position to offer Seraphina all she deserved.

SERAPHINA

"OUCH, girl. Could you try not to braid so hard, you know I'm tender headed." Junie squirmed as I gripped her thick locks.

"My bad."

"So do you think I should go with the purple wig or the fire engine red?"

"If you're looking to stand out I'd go with the red."

"You right. I'ma be the center of attention. I need to continue to dominate this summer, stay on these bitches' necks." She performed a satisfied dance with her shoulders. "So how are things with you and the mechanic?"

"It's been good." Since deciding to take our relationship to the next level, August and I were spending a lot of time together. I kept expecting to get bored of him but every time I saw him my face would light up on cue like a fireworks display. I liked him. I liked the way he would sing in the car to any and every song. Didn't matter if it was Kendrick Lamar or Cyndi Lauper. I loved that he enjoyed midnight snacking as much as I did. After making me see the stars he would cook us ramen or runny eggs butt ass naked. It was an amazing view.

I loved the way my body fit into his like a puzzle piece. My face in the crook of his neck, one leg slung over his frame as his hands gripped my thigh or played in my hair. You know that weird phase in a relationship when you don't ever want to be apart. We were there. I couldn't get enough of him when he was around, and I missed him when we weren't together.

"I like him. I think he's good for you."

"Good for me?" I grabbed the needle and thread to sew down the ends of Junie's braids.

"Yeah, it's not like I haven't noticed how different you've been since you got back home."

"Different how?" A trail of sweat slid down my face, partly because it was hot but also because I feared her next words.

"Like you experienced the worst that life had to offer in New York and you've been too scared to open yourself up to something new."

I didn't respond. I thought I was doing a good job of hiding how miserable I've been these past few months.

"It's obvi that August helps level up your dopamine."

She wasn't wrong but I wasn't interested in discussing that. "What about you? How are things going with David?" I choked out his name.

"Ugh, David and I are over. He's a grade A asshole. And I ask that you respect my privacy during this difficult time."

"You know that I can't do that." A furtive smiled played at the corners of my mouth.

"Because you're nosy."

I ripped out a big, obnoxious laugh. "Pops said the same thing a few months ago."

"Glad to hear he hasn't forgotten everything."

Running the needle and thread through her hair, I suggested, "You should come with me one Sunday."

"No thank you."

I pushed out a frustrated breath. Pops had been in the home

for a year now and I could count the number of times Junie made the effort to visit him.

"Pops would love to see you. He asks about you all the time." I fibbed.

"Bitch, I know you're lying. You've always been his favorite. He was never really checking for his other grandkids."

"That's not true." Yes, Pops and I shared a special bond but that was just because I spent time with him. One summer when I was eight, I broke my leg and spent the entire summer hanging out with Pops and we'd been close ever since. Even when I moved to New York I made a point to call him every weekend.

"It is true and it's fine. Besides, I'm not interested in seeing Pops in that gross old folks' home." Junie swatted my words away like they were a pesky mosquito.

"Summercrest isn't gross."

"The last time I was there, an old lady was screaming in the halls like something out of a horror movie."

"All done," I said, patting her on the shoulder.

Junie popped up tugging on her shorts that had crept up her thighs. "I love Pops, I do. But I just wanna remember him as he was not like what he's become."

"He hasn't changed. He's still the same old Pops."

"Old people are boring. I know we're not supposed to say shit like that but it's true." Junie bumped her shoulders.

With a wrinkle to my brow I objected, "Our elders are not boring. I've talked to Pops and several other residents of Summercrest and each one of them have lived interesting lives. I talked to a woman the other day who used to dance with Tina Turner."

Junie's face remained unimpressed.

"Tina Turner!" I repeated louder.

Junie raised her palms. "Don't kill me but I vaguely know

who that is."

"I hate you. That is exactly why I'm interviewing Pops and the others. We are losing our fucking recipes. Oral history has been around since the beginning of time. Our ancestors relied on it to pass on the stories that we weren't allowed to record. The shit they don't teach us in the outdated and inaccurate textbooks.

Today, people are actively trying to ban books about race and racism so that they can feel better about their place in this world. This is happening right now Junie, all across this country. If we don't preserve and tell our stories no one will. And that's how you end up thinking a white man invented rock and roll." The veins on the side of my neck were bulging.

"Thanks for the history lesson." Junie rolled her eyes heading to the bathroom to check out my work.

I collapsed backward onto the bed. Maybe I'd gotten a little too worked up. But this was important. Our stories, our failures and victories, our fears and desires. I felt like I was stuck in an hourglass trying to collect as much sand as I could before it all just disappeared.

Reaching for my phone, I opened Google and typed in Bernadette Gardner's name. This was probably the twentieth time I'd run this search. But seeing Pops and August's mom together sent the gears in my head spinning. I'd confirmed with August that his mother's name was in fact Bernadette. It was easy enough to secure that information without raising his suspicion.

Each time I googled her the information was always the same. Bernadette Gardner, mother of six. Wife to Augustine Gardner, Sr. Pops mentioned her husband's name was Auggie, clearly a nickname. I was able to confirm that she and Pops indeed attended the same high school and that she was married shortly after graduation. If Pops and Bernadette used to be lovers, that was a crazy coincidence. And from the looks of the cozy shoulder to shoulder laughter, the lovers may be interested in a second act.

My phone vibrated in my hand. The unexpected pulsating caused me to drop the phone on my face. I wiggled my nose to confirm I didn't break it. The vibrating was from a text message from my agent Regan in New York.

Regan: I reviewed the pages you sent me. And I really liked them.

Me: Thanks, it's still pretty rough but I think there's some interesting bits in there.

Regan: I hope you don't mind. I showed your work to the people at Rotund Press and they are very interested. They're familiar with the articles you wrote for Essence and Rolling Stone. They wanted to know if you had an appetite to turn your stories into a collection. Maybe a coffee table book or memoir?

Me: Are you joking?

I sat up staring at the screen. Had I just read that correctly?

Regan: Nope. Dead serious.

Me: Of course, I'd be interested. I'd sell my left titty for that kind of opportunity. Please don't tell them I said that.

Regan: I'll just tell them yes and set up a meeting.

Me: Regan, you're the best.

Regan: Just returning the favor. Talk to you soon.

The pages I'd send to Regan were from the hours of interviews I conducted with the senior home residents and people in my neighborhood. After each interview I asked if they were okay with me possibly sharing their stories in publication and got them to sign a release. At the time I was thinking maybe a blog or magazine feature, not a book.

I was a writer so of course writing a book was on my list of goals, but this ... I stood and took a deep calming breath. It was best I pull my head out of the clouds. When it came to getting the things I wanted, my track record was less than stellar. Even if I did get a book deal it's not like Oprah was going to add me to her book club. My phone pinged again. It was probably Regan texting back to tell me never mind. It would be just my luck that in between the two minutes we last communicated Rotund Press had a change of heart and was no longer interested in my small-town stories.

It wasn't Regan, it was August and for some odd reason the corners of my mouth tipped upward.

August: I miss you.

The subtle smile was now a full out, goofy grin. What was wrong with me. I always thought I was a gangster when it came to love, never falling too fast. Oftentimes falling long after the other party was already limping away from the impact of the fall. But August made me lose my cool. I would grow giddy with happiness whenever he crossed my mind. And August was always crossing my mind.

Me: How are things at the shop?

August: All done. Fittin' to head home. Hoping you'll meet me there?

Me: ...

August: If you want. If you have other plans that's cool too.

Me: I can be there in 30 mins. Just need to shower and change.

August: I'll order food. Wings good?

Me: Yes, that's great.

August: 😉

~

"DO you want to drive together to Summercrest?" I secretly crossed my fingers, it was gonna be in the hundreds today and I was trying to avoid melting all over my car seat.

August gave his body a good stretch as he lay beside me in his bed. "You're gonna hate me."

"After what you did last night I don't think that's possible." I teased.

"I gotta go into the shop today. There's way too much work to do and opening day is right around the corner."

I poked out my bottom lip. "I get it. It's fine. We've been dating for … what, a few weeks now and you're already neglecting me."

August rolled his body in my direction, his fingers tracing doodles on my thigh. "Neglectful? Me … never."

His hand slid into my boy shorts, his middle finger gently grazed my slit causing me to suck in air. August looked me dead in my face, delighting in my response to his touch. Opening wide, I made room so he could dip his long fingers in my honeypot. This time it was his turn to gasp for air as he met my ooey gooey center. Burying his face in my chest, he sucked on my exposed nipples before circling his tongue over my breast.

"Hey." He stopped mid finger thrust, his face lighting up. "How about you take my car to Summercrest? That way you can have an AC that actually works and a radio that plays more than one station."

"No, I couldn't, how would you get to the shop?"

"I'll take your car." He kissed the space between my breasts.

I scrunched up my face. I couldn't ask him to suffer Dorothy alone.

"It's a ten-minute drive for me. I'll be good. I'm gonna work up a sweat at the shop anyway."

"I can't."

"You can, and you will. Plus, I bet your grandpa would love a visit where you didn't smell like Funyuns the entire time."

My jaw dropped. "Are you saying I stink?"

"No, you smell great." His nostrils flared as he sniffed at me. "You taste even better." His smile turned mischievous. And just like that he disappeared in between my legs.

I loved sex at any time of day but morning sex had to be the most underrated. You're well rested and not yet drained from all the bullshit the day may bring. Feeling August's tongue flick, suck, and glide over me definitely put me in a good mood.

At Summercrest Pops wasn't up for much talking but he was eager to whip my tail in checkers. The fact that I didn't know how to play gave him a considerable advantage. I decided I was going to watch some YouTube videos so that the next time we played I could trash talk as I yelled at him to "king me."

After our visit I headed to the second floor. August had given me a photo album he wanted me to drop off with his mother. Gently rapping on the open door, Bernadette turned with a smile. She was seated at the desk in front of the window.

"What a pleasant surprise."

"Sorry to interrupt," I said, inching into her room which was decorated with floral accent pieces, including a bedspread and pillows shaped like flowers.

"Oh never you mind. I love an interruption." Bernadette waved me inside pointing to a love seat.

"August had to work but he asked me to stop by and give you this." I held up the photo album as Bernadette made her way over to the love seat to join me. Not gonna lie it was kind of weird being here without August. I'd only met his mother a handful of times, we barely knew one another.

"He works too hard. I hope you're helping him find some leisure time."

"Yes ma'am."

"So, tell me about yourself. The stuff August hasn't told me."

My eyebrows inched upward. What had August told her?

"Don't be alarmed dear. August is a man and they're never long on details. All he said was that you were pretty and smart."

"There isn't much to tell. I recently moved back to Michigan and I'm staying with my parents until I get back on my feet. I work at the Ledger, listening to other people talk."

"August told me you're a reporter."

"Yes ma'am."

"Oh, you're a quiet one. What do you and my son talk about?"

I shrugged. "Our dreams mostly. August has this amazing drive and focus and a hunger for more. I guess we're alike in that way. Hoping there's more to life than just this." I threw my hands in the air.

"I was like that too when I was your age. I married young and at some point I started to question if my life could've been more if I'd just waited, or acted. There are two types of people in this world, the ones that make stuff happen and the ones that let stuff happen."

"I definitely fall into the group that lets stuff happen."

"Why do you think that is?" She leaned in appearing to be genuinely interested in my answer.

"Because when I made stuff happen it was good for a while, but then it all came crashing down."

"Maybe you were focusing on the wrong stuff or you were in the wrong place."

"Is that what you thought when you were my age?"

Bernadette released a light, airy laugh. "I was where I needed to be. Even though the soles of my feet were itching to move."

"You had kids."

"Yes. Not so easy pursuing your dreams when you have little ones to look after."

"So what happens to your dreams?"

"The things that you neglect eventually wither and die."

That was a bleak take. Was my discontentment tied to the fact that my dreams were dying right before my eyes without me putting up a fight? I was like one of those stupid chicks after falling in a horror movie who doesn't claw their way back to a sprint, sobbing on the ground, snot faced and hyperventilating, only to be disemboweled by some psycho wearing a mask made of human flesh.

"But it's not all bad. Sometimes you just dream up new dreams."

I nod thoughtfully, having nothing of value to add.

"Franklin is your grandfather, is that right?"

"Yes. Do you two know each other?" I already knew the answer to this. I was just curious about her response.

"We go way back. We went to high school together. He was just as charming then as he is now."

"Did you two date?" If she was willing to talk, I was more than willing to listen.

Her eyes rolled to the ceiling, thoughtful. "We may have gone on a few dates but after graduation he went off to the war and I married Auggie shortly after."

It took everything in me not to yell out "Gotcha." Pops had mentioned Auggie who was clearly Augustine Senior, August's dad. My grandfather and Augustine's mother had indeed had a secret affair on and off for years. In the news biz we called this a breaking story. *After a decades long affair, old lovers are reunited.* Now that I had the confirmation I was looking for. I wasn't sure what I was going to do with this information.

It was unlikely that Bernadette would openly admit that she had been cheating on her husband for almost the entirety of their marriage. And then there was August. How do I break it to him that his mother was stepping out on his father with another man who happened to be my grandfather. Should I tell him at all? Of course, I should. I didn't like keeping secrets from people I cared about and this was a whopper.

sixteen

AUGUST

"YOU MADE THIS?" Seraphina's voice was filled with surprise.

"Yes, is that really so hard to believe?"

"I just didn't know you could cook like this."

She was referring to steak and asparagus I'd grilled in the backyard, which technically was my front yard. "I gotta continue giving you a reason to keep me around."

"I already have plenty of those." Her bare foot found my lap under the two-seater table.

"Behave." I tossed her a look.

"Do you really want that?" She massaged her toes over my dick.

"No, not really." If this woman thought I wasn't gonna finish this expensive ass filet she was mistaken. "How was Summercrest?" I asked, hoping to buy some time. I just needed to clean my plate and then she'd have my undivided attention.

She dropped her foot. "It was good. Your mother showed me your baby pictures."

"I was one cute baby." I flashed her a smile.

"Yes, you were also big as hell. Your mom said you were twelve pounds." She rubbed her brow, shaking her head.

"The Gardner family doesn't do anything small. My sisters are all five eight or taller. My dad was even taller than me at six six. But don't worry, you have wide hips so you should be fine."

Seraphina's eyes grew wide. Maybe mentioning babies to your girlfriend of four weeks was moving too fast. But I could see all that shit with her. Marriage, kids, a home that wasn't formerly used to store cars. They say when you know you know, I'd known Seraphina for a few months and I'd never been more certain of anything or anyone in my life.

"Your mother mentioned that she went to high school with my grandfather." She shifted her weight on the bar stool.

"Really? Small fucking world." I crunched into an asparagus stem that was cooked perfectly if I do say so myself.

"Yeah ... she said they even dated."

"Shut up, your gramps got good taste."

Seraphina picked at her chipped nail polish. "Pops was telling me some stories about his time with your mom. He seemed to love her. But then he went off to Vietnam."

"That sucks for your Pops but worked out nicely for my dad." I cut another piece of steak, dipping it in the mushroom sauce before popping it in my mouth.

"That's the thing." I watched as she pushed her food across her plate. "Pops said that when he came back home they reconnected."

"OK," I said, between chews.

"Pops claims the reconnection was a romantic one." Seraphina flashed me a quick glance before dropping her eyes to her plate.

"Not possible, my mom married my dad a year after graduating from high school."

"Right, but the thing is he said your mom's the love of his life."

"Really, he said that?" I didn't understand where Seraphina was going with this.

She tugged at the neckline of her T-shirt. "Yes ... and he said she loved him back."

"Hmm, didn't you say your gramps had Alzheimer's?"

Her chin descended into a reluctant nod.

"Well that's probably it. He's confused, mixing things up."

Pushing air from her nostrils she said, "Yeah ... maybe." Her eyes hollowed out taking on a far away quality.

Standing, I kissed her on the forehead before clearing our plates. When Seraphina told me her grandfather had Alzheimer's I Googled the disease, I wanted to be able to support her. During my internet search I learned that misremembering events was a common symptom. Sounds like Seraphina's grandfather saw my mom and that triggered a false memory.

My mother had been happily married to my father for years so if her granddad was suggesting anything different, he was clearly mistaken. After washing the dishes, I turned to find Seraphina in the same spot, a far off look on her face.

"Hey Sera, do you wanna get some ice cream?"

My voice pulled her from her thoughts. "You just ate a steak, loaded baked potato and asparagus and you want ice cream?"

Walking over to her I placed her hand on my dick. "I'm a growing boy."

She frowned which was not the reaction I was looking for. "You can go. I'll wait here."

My eyebrows mashed together. "No come with me. We can take your car."

"What? You want me to drive you to get ice cream, what are you five?"

A frown etched the side of my mouth. "Please, I just like having you around." I was being extra dramatic in hopes that I could persuade her.

"I'm getting the huge waffle cone with all the fixings." Hopping from the stool she grabbed her keys and we heading down the driveway toward her car. Inside I held my breath as she started the engine. The AC kicked on and cold air blew from the vents into our faces.

Seraphina placed her hand in front of the vent, her head flinching back slightly. "I think there's something wrong with my car."

"Why what's up?" I painted a concerned look on my face.

"It's blowing cold air." She blinked repeatedly.

"Isn't that what cars are supposed to do?"

"Not my car." She chuckled. "Come to think of it, Dorothy Zbornak didn't stutter and gasp when I tried to start her." Seraphina narrowed her warm, brown eyes. "What did you do?"

With a hop of my shoulders I said, "I just fixed a few things. A tune up, changed out the spark plugs, fixed the AC connectors, added some Freon."

"When, how?"

"While you were at Summercrest. I'm a mechanic. It's bad for business if my girlfriend is driving around town with a busted car. Oh, I also fixed the passenger window so you can roll it down now." I pressed the button and the glass disappeared.

Seraphina climbed over the center console and into my lap, the car engine still running. Cupping my face in her soft hands she said, "This is the nicest thing anyone has ever done for me."

A quick no jerked my head. "I doubt that."

"No, I'm serious. No one has taken care of me like you have. Thank you." Her eyes were welling with tears.

"You're welcome, baby." I thought she'd appreciate it but I

didn't anticipate tears. I don't know what type of fools she was used to dealing with but it was clear that she hadn't been loved right. It was my mission to change all of that. This woman deserved the world and I would do my best to give her as much of it as I could grab ahold of.

"I love you, August." When she blinked tears rolled down her face. "Is that OK?"

"Yeah, that's OK." Stroking the back of her neck with my hand I pulled her close, kissing her lips. "I love you too."

"Show me." Seraphina opened the passenger door climbing out, she reached for my hand leading me back toward the garage.

Stopping short I said with a laugh. "Baby, wait. Let me turn off the car. You'll come back outside and that bitch will be gone."

seventeen

SERAPHINA

I'D IGNORED the first rule of journalism, trust but verify. Pops spun a tale and I decided to run with it knowing good and damn well that he wasn't the most reliable of sources. Before I even hinted at this topic with August again I needed to vet the facts. After work I paid a visit to my grandmother Loretta. If anyone could confirm Pops's story, it would be her, having been married to him close to twenty years.

"Well look at you. What brings you to this neck of the woods?" My grandmother beamed. "Didn't think I'd see you again until next month."

"I was just passing through."

"Well come on in I got some greens and fried chicken going. Don't worry, the chicken is oven fried. I know how you young folks get with your GMO this and trans-fat that."

"When it comes to your home cooking, all that mess goes straight out the window." I reassured her.

Removing my shoes, I placed them in the cubbyhole shoe rack at the entrance. Once inside, the aroma of the hot meal she'd made enveloped me. I'd lucked out when it came to grandmothers, all three could throw down in the kitchen which made for entertaining family get-togethers. Like the time they all brought potato salad to the Juneteenth BBQ.

"How have you been, baby? Your momma told me you've been spending time with some boy."

With a smile, I nodded my head. One could only assume she was referring to August. My mom met him one time and couldn't wait to tell anyone who would listen about my little boyfriend, it was like being in high school all over again.

"Hopefully he's treating you nice."

This time my smile grew wide. I don't know how he managed it but August caused me to lose all my cool. My cynical nature, replaced by giggling fits and fizzy flutters in my stomach.

"I know that look."

"You do?" I asked.

"Yup, I felt that a time or two before."

"What happened?"

"I married him ... twice." She was talking about my grandfather. Like I said, Pops was a ladies' man and apparently the love was so good that my grandma Loretta had to go back for seconds.

"What's his name?"

"August." I tried hard not to grin like a stupid love sick teenager but it was no use.

Grandma Loretta set a plate of oven-fried chicken, collard greens, and cornbread in front of me. *Who cooks like this on a Tuesday*, I wondered.

"Tell me all about him."

For the next half hour, between bites of chicken and greens, I talked about August. I didn't even know I had ten minutes, let alone thirty of reflection associated with him but once I started it was difficult to stop. After telling my grandmother how smart, funny, and handy August was, I decided it best to get to the real reason for my visit.

"I've been visiting with Pops. He's doing well."

"I saw Franklin two weeks ago. He left me in stitches. That man is a damn fool." Pops and Grandma Loretta, while divorced, were still friendly. Grandma Loretta was his second and fourth wife. "It's nice that you go visit him as much as you do. He won't admit it but he looks forward to it."

"I do too. He's been telling me stories from his past. About his childhood and then as an adult working at that engineering firm and raising a family."

"How'd you manage getting him to share all that?"

"It took some convincing but in the end I think he kinda wanted to. He wanted to get his story out."

"Well, he has one hell of a story to tell." She poured more lemonade into my glass.

Narrowing my eyes, I critically scanned her face. "Pops mentioned a woman named Bernadette Gardner."

Grandma Loretta rolled her eyes. "Now that's a name I ain't heard in a minute."

"So you know her?"

"I know her, cussed her out, threatened to fight her, and cried on her shoulder over the course of my marriage to your grandfather."

"Why?"

"You're grown, so I'ma say it plain ... she was fucking my husband."

Houston we have lift off.

"So you knew?"

"The whole damn neighborhood knew, worst kept secret ever. The only one who didn't know was Auggie. That is until I told him."

My jaw practically unhinged at her words. "You told her

husband?" I whispered, as if someone was going to hear us in this empty house.

"She was ruining my marriage so I decided to return the favor."

"So what, Pops just had an affair with this woman for years in front of your face?"

"Sweetie, I know this may be hard to hear but your grandfather was a selfish man. He put himself first every chance he got. He married me and not one year later was hunching with that heifer. Telling me he loved me and I was the only one and for a while I believed it. But eventually I couldn't avoid the neighborhood gossip, sure I put on a brave face but your grandfather embarrassed me time and time again." All the pain she'd pushed down was now etched on her face.

"I love Franklin and because I loved him I made excuses. I tried to be the type of woman he would desire. I started fixing my hair like Bernadette's and I tried to be light and delicate like she was. God knows ain't nothing about me delicate, but I tried." She released a mirthless chuckle.

"Is that what caused you two to split?"

"No. It was the way he treated your father and uncle that was ultimately the final straw."

"What do you mean?"

"I don't think Franklin ever wanted kids. It was something people did. You get married and you start a family but he wasn't interested in raising those boys. More often than not he was at the race track, the bar, or laid up with that woman."

Pops had hinted at his lackluster parenting but my grandmother was painting a far graver picture. My father's relationship with Pops had always been strained and I never fully understood why. Pops was funny and full of life and he let me do things my parents wouldn't allow, like sneak a sip of beer or shoot an arrow.

Maybe much like my grandmother Loretta I had chosen to ignore what was right in front of my face. That my grandfather was a complicated man, and to some he was the hero while to others he was the villain. Nobody's perfect and even Pops would admit that he was flawed. It would appear that he allowed those flaws to fester, never taking the time to address the feelings of inadequacy and lack of fulfillment at home. Maybe that's why he loved Bernadette so deeply, because she accepted him, flaws and all and loved him still.

"Why'd you end up going back?"

My grandmother shrugged. "Because I loved him ... I'll love him till my last breath."

On the drive home I had much to think about. All of Pops's claims had just been confirmed. How was I going to break the news to August? Or maybe what I should be asking myself is should I even tell August about this. Knowing this information wasn't going to change anything and it could make things worse. I know I'd probably feel a way if I found out my mother had been cheating on my father for years.

I had always been too curious for my own good, that's why I became a journalist because I loved to break down the fourth wall and delve into what made people tick. Now that my curiosity was quenched it was probably best to leave this story alone. Why dig up a past no one was interested in revisiting?

eighteen

AUGUST

IN FRONT of the vending machine at Summercrest, I sorted through my change. After visiting with Seraphina's grandfather, we were now hanging out with my mother. Seraphina offered to introduce me to her grandfather on the drive over and while I was nervous, I also appreciated what this gesture meant. She trusted me and saw a future for us and she was ready to comingle our lives, which I was definitely down for.

Truth be told, I was ready to go to her place, pack her stuff and move her in. During our visit with Mr. Jacobs, he stared at me with curious eyes. He came off as a loveable grump and it was clear that Seraphina was his soft spot. I got the impression that she was fiercely protective of her grandfather and the time they spent together, so allowing me to participate was huge for her.

Also, getting to know her grandfather helped to paint a more complete picture of who she was. Franklin Jacobs wasn't short on stories, some glowing and others embarrassing, like the time she got her head caught in the rails of a banister. After the reminiscing that left my cheeks sore from laughter, we headed over to my mother's room. In true Bernadette Gardner fashion my mother's beautiful face lit up when she saw me and Seraphina walk in holding hands.

Now at the vending machine, I was getting us all soft drinks. My mother loved orange soda so I bought two so she could save one for later. I'm never one to get my hopes up but this felt good, spending time with my mother, my first love and Seraphina, who was quickly becoming the love of my life. Seraphina was amazing, what she saw in me I would never understand. But being with her made me want to work harder, which was why I was busting my ass at the shop after work and on the weekends. I couldn't offer Seraphina the world but I could pull stars from the sky so that she knew how much she meant to me.

Cold drinks in hand I approached my mother's room and overheard Seraphina asking a question.

"My grandfather mentioned that you two connected some years after graduation."

"Frankie lived across the street from us for years."

"Mrs. Gardner, do you know my grandmother Loretta Jacobs?"

"Yes, like I said they lived across the way. Frankie and his revolving door of wives."

"Well she said that you and my grandfather were closer than just neighbors."

I could hear my mother's voice hitch before she continued. "We're all so old now. It's hard to remember much of anything with any kind of certainty."

"Why are you lying?" Seraphina asked.

Entering the room, I looked at my mother's worry stricken face. "Seraphina, what the fuck are you doing?"

Seraphina jumped up from her seat, eyes wide, clearly caught by surprise that I was back so soon. "I ... I was just asking your mother a question."

"About your granddad's crazy story?"

"It's not just my granddad. My grandmother—"

"Stop it. So what, you decided you'd harass my mother?" I wasn't interested in hearing excuses. A rush of heat flushed through my body and the pounding of my heart pumped in my ears.

"No … I just want answers."

"If you're looking for answers you should start with your senile grandfather." The vein in my forehead twitched as I bared my teeth trying hard to keep my voice level, more for my mother's benefit than for Seraphina.

Seraphina's back stiffened and her eyes grew cold. "Goodbye Mrs. Gardner, it was nice seeing you again." Grabbing her purse, she shoulder checked me before leaving the room.

Everything was happening entirely too fast. Now Seraphina was mad at me but I wasn't wrong to be upset. I trusted her and she used it as an opportunity to interrogate my mother. That wasn't cool. "Mom, I'm sorry. I didn't know she was going to bring up that bullshit."

My mother nodded thoughtfully, clearly upset.

"I told her you and Dad were happily married for years and then she pulls this."

"You should go after her. Make sure she's OK."

"Are you OK?" I asked, kneeling so we were eye level.

"I'm fine. You talk to her. Go on." Her hands were shaking as she shooed me away.

Outside I found Seraphina pacing back and forth in the parking lot. She stared up at me as I approached, her face looked as if someone had just stole her puppy.

"What the fuck was that?" I tried keeping my tone even, hoping this was all some misunderstanding.

Seraphina shrugged. "I was just asking her some questions?"

"Yeah, about a story your grandfather made up during a mental break."

She brought a shaky hand to her forehead. "It's not made up. I talked to my grandmother and she confirmed it. It's not made up."

"So what are you saying, hmm? That your grandfather and my mother had what ... an affair?"

"Yes basically. Although it sounds like it was more involved than just an affair."

The pit of my stomach hardened. "Bullshit! No, bullshit. My mom loved my dad. She adored him. There ain't no way."

"Two things can be true at the same time. She could have loved your dad and been deeply connected to my grandfather."

It was as if someone took my brain and whisked it together like scrambled eggs. This was not the same woman I woke up to this morning. This was not the woman who hours ago had her legs wrapped around my waist, our bodies intertwined as she whispered how much she loved me in my ear. "That's insane, you're insane. I would know. If that happened, I would know."

"How well do any of us know our parents? Shit, I know I don't." Seraphina was reasonable and level headed, qualities I usually admired in her but right now her indifference and casual shoulder shrugs were making me heated.

"Was this your plan all along to come here and confront my mom with some shady accusation?"

"No, I planned to say nothing. I planned to let it go. But that is not how I function. I needed to know the truth."

"I thought your grandfather already gave you the truth."

"I just wanted to hear it from her. I don't know why she doesn't want to admit it—"

"Because it's not true! Damnit Seraphina, I introduce you to my mother and this is what you do?" I grimaced as pressure built behind my eyes and across my forehead.

"I understand that you're upset."

"I'm pissed. Like I don't think you get it. You literally just called my mother a fucking whore."

Seraphina's shoulders slumped, her body appearing to sag as her neck shrank. "Can you just listen to me for one second."

"Nah, we have nothing more to talk about."

"August?" She reached for me but I snatched my arm away. Disrespecting my mother, my family wasn't going to win over my heart.

"Go home Seraphina."

"OK, but you're my ride."

Now it was my turn to raise an indifferent shoulder.

"How am I supposed to get home?"

"I don't really give a fuck. Call a RideX" Turning, I headed back inside.

I ASKED MY OLDER SISTER, Deidre, to meet me at our childhood home. Actually, it was my childhood home, by the time I was born Deidre was already twenty-eight and married.

"How'd I get here before you when I live an hour away?" Deidre chided me.

"That's on you, cause you know if it ain't making me money I ain't in a rush."

Dee walked toward me, arms wide pulling me into a hug. I squeezed back just as tight. It had been months since I'd last seen her. And honestly, I just needed a damn hug. After leaving Seraphina stranded in the Summercrest parking lot, dick move I'll admit, we hadn't spoken. She called, she texted and I pretended like I hadn't listened to or read her messages dozens of times trying to figure out a way to fix this.

I missed her, but that stunt she pulled with my mother was weird. That was the only word to describe it, weirdo behavior. I'd dated my fair share of broken and damaged women, and I promised myself when I saw the signs, I wouldn't ignore them no matter how fine she was. Why Seraphina was clinging to the words of a man who oftentimes didn't know what decade he was in, was beyond me.

"You look good." Dee gave my cheek a playful smack. "So what was so important that we couldn't talk on the phone?"

Following Deidre to the living room, we took a seat on the couch.

"You know. I've been visiting Mom in that ... place and I've just started thinking there's so much I don't know about her ... about Dad."

"Well you were always in your own little world. Buildings could collapse all around you and you wouldn't have a clue."

"That's because I know how to mind my business."

"Isn't your family your business?" Dee wrinkled her round nose at me.

I shrugged her comment off. "I guess ... I was just ... Mom and Dad were happy ... right?

For the most part. I remember them being in love. Like madly in love. My dad would come home from work and scoop my mother in his arms, dipping her at the waist before planting a kiss on her lips. Some evenings I'd find them in the living room cheek to cheek, dancing to soft jazz music.

"They were happy enough. But no couple's perfect."

"Was Mom happy?"

"Where's all this coming from Auggie?"

How do you explain that your girlfriend, the reporter, may have uncovered a family scandal? Shit none of this made sense and I didn't know if Seraphina still considered herself my girlfriend after I jumped down her throat this past Sunday.

"Mom just said something the last time I visited that threw me off." I lied. Telling the truth would be too complicated and then I'd have to mention Seraphina and Dee would ask questions about her that I didn't have answers for right now.

"You know I always got the sense that Mom made the best of the situation she found herself in. She wasn't unhappy but she wasn't completely fulfilled if that makes sense?"

"With life in general or Dad?"

"Maybe a bit of both."

I scrubbed my face with my hand. "Did she ... was there someone else?"

"Are you sure you wanna get into this stuff?"

"Yea, of course I do. I'd prefer the truth rather than some fucked up fairy tale."

Dee took a deep breath like she was bracing herself for impact. "There was a man. He lived across the street from us in the house before this one. I just remember there were a lot of long stares and covert smiles between them. One weekend I think it was the Fourth of July or something because Mommy and Daddy were hosting a party. You remember they loved to entertain."

I nodded.

"Anyway, the whole neighborhood was over and hanging out in the backyard. I went upstairs to get a book or something and I saw them in Mom and Dad's bedroom kissing. I think I must have gasped because Mom saw me looking. She begged me not to tell Daddy. She said it wasn't what it looked like." Dee shot me a stare. "I was young but I knew a passionate kiss when I saw it. I watched All My Children religiously."

"Maybe it *was* just a misunderstanding. You were a kid you couldn't be sure of what you were seeing."

"I was fourteen and I know what I saw."

Other than claiming that I was adopted Deidra had never lied to me. "What did you do?"

"I kept her secret. I was happy to pretend it never happened."

"So you never spoke about it ... ever?"

"No."

"Who was the man ... that Mom was kissing?"

"Mr. Jacobs. He was married too at the time so it was just a mess."

Jacobs, that was Seraphina's last name. Fuck.

"Was Dad cheating too?"

"I don't know. If he was, I never caught him."

"Wow."

"I know it's a real mind fuck when you find out your parents aren't who you thought they were."

"Did you tell anyone else?"

"Not then but over the years I've told the others."

"So wait, everyone knows but me?" I could feel the familiar tingling as my ears grew hot from anger.

"Yes."

"And you didn't think that was something I should know?"

Deidra raised a cautious eyebrow. "You know how you get."

"No, what does that mean? How do I get?"

"You just take things to heart. You're sensitive in that way."

I loved my sisters but I was so sick of them treating me like a child. Yes, I was the baby of the family but we were all adults now and I should be included in decisions and told important information. They excluded me from the Summercrest discussion and apparently important details about my parents were considered need-to-know information for everyone but me.

"This is bullshit and you know it. You should have told me."

All Deidre offered was a blasé shoulder shrug. "Follow me." After heading upstairs, my sister rummaged around in my mother's closet. The last time I was in her bedroom was right before my father's funeral when she helped to fix my tie. She told me everything was going to be OK and I told her I would take care of her. My chest ached at the realization that both our words were lies.

"Here," she said, exiting the closet and holding out a stack of letters held together with a yellow ribbon.

"What is this?"

"You said you want to know the truth. Well, here it is in black and white and doodles of hearts with arrows through them."

I pulled the top envelope from the stack. On the front was scribed, "To my dearest Bernadette."

nineteen

SERAPHINA

LAYING on my bed staring at the ceiling summed up the trajectory of my life. This bedroom was like a type of purgatory. I was stuck between two worlds: the old world of my youth and this new world that was slowly unfolding. A new world that no longer included August after I imploded my relationship because I couldn't mind my damn business. It had been a week. I texted. I called. I even did the dreaded drive by. All my efforts went unanswered. He was mad and clearly through with me which I got because I was also over my bullshit.

My phone rang pulling me from my thoughts. "Hello?"

"Are you sitting down?" Regan, my agent's familiar voice rang out from the other end.

"Yep," I said, releasing a long breath bracing myself for the inevitable disappointment that was surely about to follow.

"I just got off the phone with Rotund Press and they want to sign you to a book deal."

I examined my phone screen double checking that this was not a prank call. "Come again."

"Rotund Press is in, all in. You killed the virtual meeting.

They couldn't stop raving about how refreshing and smart you were. One of them said they loved your dry wit."

"My dry wit?"

"Yeah, I thought the same thing and had to confirm they were talking about you."

"What does this mean?"

"This means an advance, a generous one. They found your blog. Why didn't you tell me that your blog had over a half a million active followers?"

I shrugged even though she couldn't see me.

"I didn't even know people still read blogs. That coupled with your writing portfolio has landed you a six-figure advance my friend."

I dropped the phone, tilted my head and banged on my ear. There must be something lodged in there because I thought I just heard her say six figures.

"Are you still there?" Regan asked.

"Yeah, I'm still here."

"Did I wake you up from a nap or something? You are about to be paid. I'm gonna need a little more excitement."

"I'm totally excited. This is my excited voice." I was excited but skeptical, things always had a funny way of bottoming out underneath me. Exhibit A. My relationship with August.

"OK, well treat yourself to a nice meal or a massage because you deserve it. I'll send over the contract when I get it. Congrat-ulations."

"Thank you. Talk to you soon." Ending the call I stared at the face of my phone in disbelief. *Had that just happened or did I just imagine it? I should tell ...* The person I really wanted to tell wasn't talking to me and it was looking less likely he ever would. Shit. Pushing the thoughts from my head I forced myself to focus on the positive. Like the fact that this advance could get me out of my parents' house. If that wasn't cause for celebration, I don't know what was. Lifting myself from the bed, I decided to treat myself just like Regan suggested, with ice cream.

In the kitchen I scooped out a generous serving of chocolate-brownie-fudge ice cream, just as I was about to savor the first spoonful, the doorbell rang. I wasn't expecting visitors and my parents were gone for the day on some antique roadshow vibe. Even after all these years of marriage they still enjoyed doing things together, which to me was the sign of a healthy marriage. But don't hold me to that theory because my relationship success rate was a big fat zero.

Rising from the kitchen table, I treaded to the door swinging it open, August's frame was on the other side blocking out the sun. My cheeks grew warm at the sight of him. Thank God for this melanin-rich skin, it hid the flush that had crept over my face.

"Hi," he said.

"Hi."

August rubbed the back of his neck. "Can we talk?"

I resisted the urge to be petty and remind him that I'd been ready to talk. He was the one who'd been acting like a child ignoring my attempts to hash shit out. Stepping aside, I allowed him to enter. *Oh my God he smells divine. Can he just apologize so we can fuck already?*

"I've been thinking about what happened between us last Sunday."

Uh-oh, no good conversation ever started with the words "I've been thinking."

Standing in the foyer, August looked at the ceiling more than my face. "I fucked up. And making you find your own way home was not my finest moment. I was upset and you were saying a lot of stuff and it was difficult for me to wrap my head around it all."

"I shouldn't have confronted your mother."

"No, you shouldn't have." His expression was rigid, the muscle in his jaw working in a tight circle. At least we were on the same page about that one point. It was wrong of me to ambush his mom. I could admit that.

The grandfather clock in the living room loudly ticked away the time as we stood in silence waiting for the other to make the first move. Maybe I should offer a more formal apology? We were in this awkward situation because of me. I readied my mouth to speak but August beat me to it.

"You were right."

"About what?"

"Everything ... all of it." August scrubbed his face with his hands. "I talked to my sister, Deidre. Dee is the oldest. I figured if anyone knew about this alleged affair it would be Dee."

"And did she?"

"She witnessed my mom and your grandfather kissing ... passionately."

"When?"

"Years ago, she was a kid. My mom caught her watching and begged her not to say anything and Dee kept her secret."

"All these years?"

"Apparently so." August shrugged. "There's also this." August pulled out a stack of letters from his back pocket.

Opening one of the letters, I skimmed the contents filled with words of longing and desire and plans of forever signed "With all my love for all my life, Frankie." August's eyes were tired and pained, clearly still processing what all this meant for the shattered image of his parents as a happy, married couple.

"Where did you get these?" I shook the stack of love notes in my hand.

"Dee found them a while back when my sisters were sorting

through Mom's stuff, trying to decide what to trash and what to keep."

I tugged at the corner of a photograph in the middle of the stack. Pulling it free from the pile, I set the letters down on the foyer table to examine the photo. A young Pops and Bernadette, wrapped in one another's arms, Pops nuzzling her neck all smiles. Maybe they were in their thrities, maybe younger. It's always harder to gauge age when it comes to black folks.

"I'm sorry, August. I wish it weren't true."

"No need for sorrys you tried to tell me and I wouldn't listen. I also said some pretty fucked up shit about your grand-father and his condition. It was insensitive and mean. I wish I could take that shit back. I was upset but that didn't mean I had the right to be an asshole. I'm sorry, I know your granddad is important to you and I should have been more thoughtful in the words I chose." I could tell from his pained expression that he was trying to make this right.

"Thank you, I appreciate that."

August continued, "You were right ... all I know about my parents ... shit all we know about anyone is what they show us. And my parents chose to *act* like a happy, loving couple but those letters paint a different story."

"Maybe they were. If there is one thing that I know for certain it's that life is complicated and things are not always cut and dry."

August fixed his gaze onto mine, slowly inching forward until the space between us was eliminated. "Did I fuck this up?" His rugged hand cupped my face, brushing my cheek with his thumb.

"No, I'm still very much pro August."

Dropping his hand from my cheek, he wrapped his arm around my waist lifting me off my feet with ease.

"Upstairs." I whispered between kisses.

On the landing August asked, "Which way?"

"To the right." I pointed toward my open bedroom door.

There was a cyclone of clothes as we rushed to undress one another. It had only been a week but I missed his touch. The way he manipulated my body, the way he liked to kiss my mouth when he came, so that his moans echoed inside of me. With the condom in place, I climbed on top slowly lowering myself as he entered. I worked my hips over his lap taking full control, wanting him to feel how sorry I was and how much I'd missed him.

August rubbed his bearded face between my chest before capturing a breast in his mouth. He rolled his tongue over my nipples and areola as I wiggled my backside in a swirling motion. His steady hands on my waist helped lift me to the tip of his shaft before I crashed back down. Each downward slide stealing my breath. Leaning back, I braced myself, hands against his knees, I rocked back and forth in an attempt to drive him deeper inside of me.

Pulling me from his lap, he draped me over the edge of the bed taking me from behind.

As he slid into place I called for him. "August, yes." And with each thrust the afternoon light turned to night because all I could see were stars. The red giant star, white dwarf, and finally a supernova that pulsated my core leaving me wet, sticky, and throbbing.

As the morning transitioned into afternoon, I lay curled up in August's arms, my head resting on his chest, staring out the window. "What are you going to do about your mom?"

"I'm gonna talk to her. I want answers. If my childhood was a lie I think I deserve to know."

August's hand absentmindedly stroked my arm.

"If you need me to be there just say the word."

"Really?" His eyebrows inched upward in surprise.

"Absolutely." I straddled him. "Don't let it go to your head but I would probably walk over hot coals for you."

Sitting up, August brushed my coily curls from my face. "Move in with me."

"What?" I needed to make sure this wasn't the lingering after effects of bomb sex. I myself had been known to say some crazy things after a man brought me to a satisfying release.

"I've been thinking about this for a while."

"A while? We've only known each other for four months."

"Four glorious months. Four months that confirmed what I already knew the second I met you. That this girl could be the one."

"Bullshit, when we met you were more concerned with pummeling that vending machine than wooing me."

"Yes, but when you walked away I was like who was that?"

"Because of my dazzling personality?"

"Mostly because of your ass but your personality was a close second."

I snorted out a goofy laugh. "Very funny."

"Seriously, I love you Sera and I don't need more time. I just wanna be with you ... every day. Maybe I'm moving too fast but life is meant to be lived and I've never been one to play games. I know what I want ... FYI it's you, in case I'm not making myself clear." His hands tickled my spine as he ran them up and down.

"I love you too." A smile contorted my face. "Is this crazy?"

"Well you have to be a little crazy to fall in love."

He was right about that, you had to be slightly cuckoo for cocoa puffs to love someone. Love was essentially the spiritual embodiment of opening yourself up and allowing someone to move in. August took up space inside my heart and my head and caused my motor functions and internal organs to malfunction whenever he was near.

"Yes, let's do it." I cupped his face in my hands. "Fair warning on hair wash day I'm gonna use all the hot water."

"That's cool. I grew up with sisters. I completely respect the importance of wash day."

"I'm gonna hog the covers." I stroked the side of his bearded cheek.

"We'll buy more."

"And I tend to be extremely horny first thing in the morning, and in the middle of the day ... oh and right before bed." My hips subconsciously grinded against his lap causing his dick to once again come alive.

"You won't hear me complaining, I assure you." Flipping me on my back he whispered over my mouth. "So we doing this?"

"We are definitely doing this." I said, pressing my lips to his.

twenty

AUGUST

SERAPHINA PLACED her hand on my knee which was hopping up and down signifying my nerves. We were in the garden at Summercrest that looked more like a small park with walking paths and a pond with three turtles named Frank, Dean, and Sammy. Named after Frank Sinatra, Dean Martin, and Sammy Davis Jr., a fact my mother shared with me during one of our visits. Which was followed by me heading straight to Google to figure out who the hell she was talking about.

We invited my mother to join us in the garden. Seraphina and I agreed on the car ride over that we wouldn't accuse her of anything, we would just tell her what we knew and give her the opportunity to explain. I was already prepared for my mother to be defensive based on her cagey response when Seraphina went all Nancy Drew on her last Sunday.

"It's gonna be fine." Seraphina reassured me.

"What if it's not? What if she gets mad?"

"Why would she get mad?"

"Because quite honestly this shit is none of our business."

She grabbed my chin tilting it down so that our eyes met.

"Listen, I'll follow your lead. If you don't want to bring it up then don't."

"I just wanna know the truth. I don't want my mother to have to hold on to these secrets. I'm gonna love her regardless. Am I disappointed yeah but her relationship with my dad is separate and apart from me." I scratched at my beard. "Maybe we should let this shit go."

"OK." Seraphina agreed.

If she was disappointed I couldn't tell. And there was no time to figure it out as my mother appeared with Seraphina's grandfather at her side heading toward us. *What the hell is he doing here?*

"Well isn't this a nice change of pace?" My mother said, leaning in for a hug she whispered in my ear. "Glad to see you two worked things out."

While my mother and Seraphina exchanged pleasantries, I shook Mr. Jacobs's hand. "Nice to see you again sir."

"Good to be seen, Augustine." He gave my shoulder a quick pat.

Augustine was my father's name and hearing him speak it made my skin crawl. I told Seraphina I wanted to get to the truth. What I hadn't told her was that I wasn't a fan of her grandfather and even though he was an old man I was tempted to punch him square in the jaw. He deserved that and more for all the time spent interfering in my parents' marriage.

"You look pretty in that color dear. Complements your skin tone," my mother said.

Seraphina ran her hand over her orange dress. "Thank you."

"Luckily she got her looks from her mother's side of the family." Mr. Jacobs chimed in.

My mother rested her hand on his arm. "Don't go selling yourself short. You were a real looker back in the day … still are."

Heat evaded my ears and neck as I clenched my fist hoping to contain my anger. Seeing my mother flirting with that man made my blood boil. I quickly abandoned all thoughts of letting this go.

Releasing a tight-lipped huff, I slammed the stack of love notes onto the table. "What is this?"

My mother looked from the stack to my expectant face and back again. "It looks like mail, dear."

Was this how she was able to get away with this for all these years, just dismissing anyone who got too close to the truth? Deidre, my father, Seraphina, and now me.

"Yeah mail between you and Mr. Jacobs. Letter after letter about secret rendezvous and burning desire."

"You kept the letters I wrote you?" The old man looked at my mother with such softness in his eyes.

"Of course I did." My mother's tone was as smooth as silk until she turned to me. "So is this why you threw me into this home so you could snoop through my things?"

"I didn't put you here. You can thank your daughters for that. And I wasn't snooping, Deidre found them when she was looking for your will and other important papers."

My mother and I rarely argued. I was an unashamed, momma's boy through and through, so the rising tension was causing me heartburn.

"My private papers are none of your business, Augustine. A child should always remember their place."

"But I'm not a child. I'm a grown man asking my mother to stop lying to me."

"I never lied to you."

"You're right, you lied to all of us ... Dad, Dee, Janette ... all of us." I was yelling now which I hoped not to do but I couldn't control the hurt that was brewing deep inside. I really only had three moods ... happy, angry, or indifferent.

"He's certainly got his father's temper." The old man said, coughing out a laugh.

I was going to get arrested for elder abuse because I was two seconds away from knocking gramps off his block.

Seraphina reached for me, holding my hand in her warm, soft embrace helped some of the pressure that was building to evaporate. "We didn't come here to argue, we just wanted to understand. This relationship which is obviously very important to both of you doesn't have to be a secret any longer. If you want us to stop meddling I understand and we can drop this topic and talk about something more agreeable like the Pistons."

"The Pistons suck. Next topic." The old man said, at least we agreed on one thing.

My mother clasped her hands. "What do you want to know?"

"Why'd you lie?"

"Sweetie, it isn't that simple."

"Sure it is. You lied for years. You weren't happy and you stayed. Why?"

"It was a different time. Women didn't just leave. And your father was a difficult man."

My fist banged the table. "Don't do that. Don't paint my dad as the villain."

"There is much about your father that you don't know."

"Did he hit you?"

"No."

"Did *he* cheat?"

"No."

"Then I know everything I need to know about my father."

"August, maybe we just let her explain." Seraphina suggested.

My mother flashed Seraphina an appreciative smile. "When

Frankie went off to the war I was devastated. So many of our young men ... boys really ... were dying over there and I feared that he would suffer the same fate. I met your father and he was strong and confident, much like you and I fell hard. We got married and started a family."

"But apparently that wasn't enough." I sneered.

Ignoring my reprimand she continued. "When Frankie returned from the war I was a different person, we both were. We'd both been through our fair share of hurt and disappointment. But seeing Franklin again renewed my belief in things working out as they should. I never intended for our friendship to morph into something deeper but it did. I loved your father but—"

I snorted out a laugh rubbing my eyes. "That's not how love works."

"Are you looking for an explanation or are you looking to assign blame?"

"I already got the blame part figured out. I'm just looking for some type of rational justification."

My mother turned to Seraphina. "August has always been a choir boy. He only sees the world in black and white, good and evil. For August, there is no middle ground, there is no gray area. He's been like this since birth."

I hitched my shoulder in disbelief. Was she really gonna talk about me like I wasn't here? There was no moral gray area when it came to cheating. It should never happen. Period. Was this the same woman who taught me to respect my elders and the importance of keeping my word now back pedaling? We are what we do, not what we say. My father taught me that.

Seraphina spoke up. "I think that August is just having a difficult time reconciling what he saw at home every day and the stark realization that this happy family who ate dinner together every night and played board games may not have been so picturesque. To hear August tell it you guys were like the Huxtables."

Turning to her I gave her a thank you nod. Seraphina was far better at words than I was. And when I was angry it was even harder for me to articulate my thoughts.

"Your father and I wanted you kids to have structure and a solid support system. The world is rough and cruel but your home shouldn't be."

"Mom, I'm trying to understand but I don't. So what ... did you and Dad just pretend you were happy for us?"

"Son, it's not right to put all the blame on your mother." Mr. Jacobs chimed in. "Bernadette left my heart in pieces so many times. Calling it quits saying we were over and that she needed to focus on her family. And for a time she would stick firm to it but the heart doesn't work that way. You can't just shut your feelings off like a light switch.

"I'm the first to admit that what we did was wrong. Shoot, I was married to a fine woman and I put her through hell. I ain't proud of it and she didn't deserve none of it. I love Bernadette, this is true but I truly regret the people we hurt while we were caught up in the middle of that love. The people we are still hurting. I'm sure my apology is worth less than dirt to you but I am sorry for the pain our relationship caused."

I'm not gonna sit here and lie saying that his apology made it better. But what was I supposed to do, ice my mother out of my life because I didn't agree with her choices, which before a few days ago I was totally unaware of.

"August you still seem upset honey." My mother wrapped her delicate hand around mine.

"Yeah, that's not going away any time soon. What you do with your life is none of my business. Who you choose to spend time with, the people you choose to deceive, those are your choices and you have to live with them, not me." Standing, I addressed Seraphina, "I'm gonna wait in the car."

I didn't turn back when Seraphina called out asking me to return to the table. I was done. This was a mistake, all of it. If I had a time machine, I'd set the dial back to before I knew any of this. Maybe my whole childhood was a lie but the memories felt real.

The way my mother's face lit up when my father entered a room. The way my father would sneak into the kitchen and pretend to steal us cookies while my mother cooked. The entire time I would giggle loudly thinking my father was a master cookie thief. I believed their love story because I felt it every day all around me. How was that all made up?

SERAPHINA

THE RIDE HOME was quiet with August stewing in his anger and hurt and me letting him have his moment. Back at his place he moved around the small space looking for something to do. Straightening the comforter, washing our dishes from breakfast, and taking out the trash. Anything so that he wouldn't have to process his feelings.

"I'm gonna make us some sandwiches," he said, pulling the mustard and mayo from the fridge.

"So do you wanna talk about it?"

"Talk about what? You don't want sandwiches? I'm easy, we could order something."

"Sandwiches are great. What happened back at Summercrest not so much."

"Honestly, Seraphina I don't care. Everything's coming up roses for me. I've got you and the shop opening in a few weeks. I'm good."

"I will agree that having me makes you a really lucky man." I pressed my hand to his heart. "But you don't have to be good. It's OK to feel some type of way about this whole situation."

"But I don't." His tone implied finality.

"OK." My shoulders sank into a rounded heap.

"OK." He flooded my cheek with kisses before grabbing the loaf of bread. Clearly, content in pretending that everything was alright.

This was all my fault. I should never have told him about the affair. He was happy and spoke about his parents' marriage like it was relationship goals and I ruined all that for him because I was careless and as always didn't think before throwing on my deerstalker hat like Sherlock Holmes.

My heart clambered up my throat. "I'm sorry. I didn't mean for any of this to happen."

August didn't look up from the turkey slices he was arranging on the bread. "It's not your fault."

"It is. You can blame me. I'd actually prefer it because it's one hundred percent my fault."

"For telling me the truth?" His eyes rested on me soft and heartfelt.

"So you're not mad at me?" I bit my lip in an attempt to contain the tears I was trying to hold at bay.

"Baby, why would I be mad at you?" He pulled me in, cupping my face in his hands.

"I can think of several reasons, but the most prominent is the fact that I inserted myself into something that was none of my business. And when Pops told me about him and your mom I could have just kept it pushing."

"You could have but that's not your MO; you're a nosy son of a bitch."

"I really am." I whimpered as a rascal tear escaped my ducts.

"That's what I love about you. You ask questions. You don't accept things for what they are, you have a curious mind."

"It's a thirst for knowledge." I teased, finally allowing my shoulders to relax.

Kissing my lips softly he pressed his forehead to mine. "I love you, we're cool. Now my mother, that's a different story." Releasing me he returned to the sandwiches. "Do you want the fancy mustard or plain?"

"Fancy." Chewing on the inside of my cheek, I debated whether I should say anything further, after all I was done sticking my nose where it didn't belong. Fuck it, I wasn't known for biting my tongue. "Can I just say one more thing?"

August's silence was my green light to proceed.

"Don't let your anger cloud your better judgment. You said it yourself life is short and you don't want that anger to fester and ruin the years you have left with your mother. Because that kind of regret, words unsaid, hurts unmended can't be undone. And I don't want that for you."

August nodded thoughtfully before cutting our sandwiches in half, taking a big bite.

AFTER SPENDING several nights in a row at August's place, I decided to make an appearance at home. Partly, because I needed a clean pair of drawers, but mainly because I wanted to give August the space to think without my influence. These past weeks he'd been inundated with information, it was gonna take a minute to fully digest it all.

"Seraphina is that you?" My father called from the living room.

Of course it was me. Who else would it be, Glinda the Good Witch?

"Hey guys how's it going?" I asked, finding my parents playing a game of Scrabble.

"You've been MIA the past few days. I hope you're not over-staying your welcome at Junie's place," my mother said.

Life was moving so fast that I hadn't updated my parents on much of anything really. The past few weeks especially had us like ships passing in the night, when I was coming, they were going. I hadn't told my parents about August, the book deal, or the shit with Pops.

I released a long sigh. "Yeah about that. I'm moving out."

"With Junie?" My father lifted an eyebrow. "I give that a month."

Pulling a chair up to the folding table they'd erected to play their word game, I continued. "Not Junie. I'm moving in with August."

My mother removed her reading glasses. "August, I thought you said he stayed in a garage?"

"He does, but it's essentially a studio apartment." Make no mistake it was a damn garage but I was OK with that.

My father dropped his tiles. "Now wait a minute. Who the hell is August?"

You remember Herman, I told you about that fella who showed up asking after Sera."

My dad pushed his glasses up the brim of his nose. "Seraphina honey, how long have you known this guy? Moving in is a big step."

What my parents didn't understand was that I wasn't asking for permission or approval. I was just being a good tenant providing them notice that at the end of the month my room would be vacant.

"I understand it's a big step and we both agree we're ready to make it ... together."

"What's this about a garage? The stuff in your room alone will clutter up that garage."

"It'll be fine. The garage is temporary."

"What's his last name?" My father asked, normally my mother was the one with twenty questions but for some reason my dad's interest was piqued. "Where are his people from?"

"Gardner, August Gardner. And his family is from Michigan." My mouth curved into a smile when his name crossed my tongue.

"Gardner? As in Bernadette Gardner's son?" My mom chimed in tossing my father a curious eye.

"That's a blast from the past. Bernadette Gardner is not a friend of this family." My father's face turned bitter. "You spend all that time with your grandfather, you should ask him about Mrs. Gardner. You'd get an earful."

"I know all about Pops and Mrs. Gardner and that has absolutely nothing to do with August and I." The last thing I was going to do was be dragged into the standing family feud between the Jacobs and the Gardners. While I understood that my father held animosity toward the woman he blamed for ruining his parents' marriage I wasn't actively chasing this tale any longer. I'd learned all I needed to know and this was one story I was happily laying to rest.

"Well, just make sure he's not married."

"Herman, that's enough." My mother chided.

"I'm just saying the Gardners care very little about the sanctity of marriage and vows made before God and all that." He pinned his arms over his chest.

"Last time I checked it took two to tango." I scoffed off my father's words.

Who knew that the Gardner name was forbidden in this household? My father's features tightened. And in that moment, it dawned on me that he'd had a front row seat to all the mayhem Pops and Bernadette's affair caused. Certainly, my dad watched as his parents argued; he probably had to comfort Grandma Loretta on more than one occasion when the weight of it all became too much for her to conceal. Was love worth it if it meant hurting so many people?

Pops apologized to August today but I still wondered if he and Mrs. Gardner fully understood the hurt their choices caused. If they even cared. August planned to make another trip to Summercrest and I was hopeful he'd receive what he needed to help him process this unexpected information and move forward.

When he talked to his mother, I'd be there to support him in any way he needed. And I had to admit I was just as interested in getting answers as he was. Was it worth it? Did they have regrets? Would they do it all again knowing what they now know? August may not be in need of closure but others were, including my father.

"KNOCK, KNOCK." I entered my mother's room, finding her in her usual spot by the window. The way her face lit up when she saw me made me feel even worse about my temper tantrum last weekend.

"I didn't expect to see you again so soon. Last time we spoke you were mighty upset."

"I was but I've had some time to think." Pulling up a chair I took a seat across from her. "I'm not proud of how I acted and I wanted to apologize. What went on between you and Mr. Jacobs is none of my business. You were right, I'm stubborn but I'm learning to let stuff go."

"Augustine, my darling boy. Do you know why I love you so much?"

I shook my head left to right.

"Because of your integrity. And your unwavering desire to be a good man. Your father was like that. I didn't always appreciate it. I'd tell him I needed excitement and adventure. I was a social butterfly and your father preferred staying home. That's why I've always tried to ingrain into you and your sisters the importance of finding someone who matches your speed, so that no one ever gets left behind."

She was right, Seraphina and I both preferred being alone. And being alone with her just felt right because I could be my authentic self when I was with her. I didn't have to have all the answers or constantly play it cool. Shit, she watched me cry over the cartoon movie *Encanto*.

My favorite part of the day was when we curled up on the couch while I watched sports center and she read a book, sneaking in kisses during the commercial breaks. Or our newest Sunday routine, making breakfast together while Ari Lennox or Jhene Aiko sang in the background.

I'd always been a relationship type of guy. The year before meeting Seraphina was the longest I'd ever been single. I just love the comfort of having my person, I'm simple that way. I love the mundane relationship shit. I'd take playful arguments over where to eat over the bullshit getting-to-know-you phase any day. Me suggesting Thai, Mexican, or pizza with Seraphina hemming and hawing over what she's in the mood for before vetoing each one.

My mother continued. "I get it, you see me as the woman who kissed your boo boos and put sweet notes in your lunch box but I'm not just your momma, Augustine. I had dreams and desires long before you were a twinkle in my eye."

I nodded my head thoughtfully. I was taken back to a conversation that Seraphina and I had months ago about who our parents were before us. I'd never given it much consideration but now looking into my mother's brown eyes, I was realizing for the first time there was so much I didn't know. She'd lived almost half her life before she even had me so how could I expect to know everything about her.

"I made amends to your father years ago. And a few years

before you were born Franklin and I ended things for good. And then we moved out of the city. And your father and I worked hard to put the past behind us. So, no your childhood wasn't a lie. The love I had for your father was very real."

"You don't have to explain anything to me. I'm sorry about all this. Seraphina and I both are. She wanted you to know she wasn't trying to stir up trouble." Leaning forward I cradled my mother's hands in mine. "I'm all in with her and I need you to love her just as much as I do."

Being a momma's boy it was important that my mother and Seraphina get along. I didn't want the events over the past few weeks to sour my mom on what an amazing person Seraphina was.

"All I've ever wanted is for you to find someone who made you happy and I can see that Seraphina is up for the job. If you like it, I love it. Is that what you young folks say?"

I chuckled. "Yeah Mom, exactly that."

"I like her. She's a bit nosy but I like her." My mother teased.

I breathed a sigh of relief. That was really all that mattered now. The past was in the past, my focus was on my future with Seraphina.

"Who knows, maybe we can go on a double date sometime," she said.

"So you and Mr. Jacobs ..."

"If all these years on this earth have taught me anything it's that life is short. And now that I'm in my golden years the sand seems to slip even faster through the hourglass. I want to live the time I have left with the people I love the most. And yes, Frankie is one of those people."

Hearing that was unexpected but I meant it when I said my mother's choices were none of my business. I don't have to understand them or agree with them. "I just want you to be happy, Mom. That's all I've ever wanted."

"And that I am. Seeing my kids thriving and finding their place in this world makes me happy. Knowing that for all my faults maybe I did one thing right."

Kissing my mother's cheek I reassured her. "I love you Mom and I'm happy we're both finding our happy ending."

twenty-three

"CAN I just say that at y'all's big age you should have hired movers. Don't no one wanna lug heavy boxes up and down stairs all morning." Junie complained as she shoved a box into the back of Sly's truck.

"We're trying to save money," I said, following behind her with a box of my own.

"Girl you just got that huge book advance you can splurge."

"Nope, splurging is what forced me to move back in with my parents a year ago. Lesson learned. Besides, August and Sly are here to do the heavy lifting."

"I've got something heavy for Sylvester to lift." Junie giggled, sticking out her tongue.

I don't even know why she was making a fuss. I only had a few boxes. The majority of my things would remain at my folk's place until August and I figured out a more permanent solution.

"This is the last of it," August said, carrying two medium-sized boxes. I attempted to grab one but he shooed me away, arranging them into the truck bed with ease.

"If you're having second thoughts you need to speak now. Because once I get settled into your place I'm never leaving."

He bopped my nose with the tip of his finger. "Our place."

A blush crept over my face. August was like a diamond in the rough. Like a first edition collection of short stories signed by Langston Hughes that was sold for pennies on the dollar because the seller didn't recognize what they had. I vowed to never be that careless and let the masterpiece that was August Gardner get away from me.

Stretching to my tiptoes, I softly kissed his lips. August returned my kiss with one of his own. With a gentle tug he pulled me upward and I wrapped my legs around his waist. It was only noon but I never missed an opportunity to feel his strong, muscular frame against mine. You know when you're out and about and you see a couple passionately kissing in public in the middle of the day and then someone yells out "Get a room"? August and I were the couple in need of a room so that no one else had to witness our desperate and futile attempts to inhabit the same body.

"Eww, so you two just gonna suck face in front of your momma and daddy's house like that?" Junie asked.

Junie's voice brought me back to the present point in time. Loosening my grip from around his waist, I planted my feet solidly on the floor. "Sorry, we were just—"

"In love ... I get it. It's disgusting. But I get it." She teased.

"We good?" Sly asked, wiping a sheen of sweat from his brow.

"Yep, we're ready to roll."

Sly shot a glance at Junie. "Do you wanna ride with me?"

Junie's face pulled into a huge smile. "Sure." Making her way to the passenger side, she climbed in.

"We're right behind you." August shook his car keys in his hand.

I headed back inside to say goodbye to my mom and dad. They were in the kitchen snacking on cheese and crackers.

"I'm heading out." I announced.

"Did you get everything you need? You should take extra blankets because you get cold when the weather cools. Does August have warm blankets?" My mother asked, standing she headed upstairs.

"Please remind Mom that I'm just moving ten minutes away." I said to my dad.

"You're her baby and she is always gonna fuss over you. We both are." He gave my hand a squeeze. "Your mom and I are proud of you and August seems like a nice guy, even if he's a Gardner."

I ignored that last part. I couldn't expect my father to move past what Pops and Mrs. Gardner did. And after sticking my nose where it didn't belong, I'd decided to focus on the business that paid me. Which, with my hefty advance from Rotund Press, was now compiling all the stories I'd collected this year from the residents at Summercrest, the neighbors in the community, and the random people who struck up conversations with me and five minutes later were knee deep into their life story.

My mother returned with an armful of blankets both quilted and crocheted. "Better to have them when you need them."

"Thank you." Giving my folks big hugs I made my way back to August's Chevy where he was scrolling on his phone. After setting the blankets in the back seat, I opened the passenger door and settled in.

"Did your mother cry?"

"She's still gonna see me all the time. This is a happy day not a sad one." I clicked my seatbelt into place.

"I'm happy because I'll get to wake up to your face every morning."

"You don't think we're moving too fast?"

"If this shit with my mother has taught me anything it's

that life is meant to be lived. I don't wanna wait for the right time, whatever the hell that means. I wanna love you loudly right now in this moment and all the moments to come. And I hope you want that too."

"No games?"

"I suck at games … I have a terrible poker face."

"OK, let's take the guard rails off and start living." Leaning forward, I gave his lips a quick peck.

Since returning home I'd been going through the motions. Smiling when expected, showing up to events but not really experiencing them. Meeting August changed all that. I was no longer trying to speed life up to get to the good parts. Every moment with him was a memory I wanted to bask in and enjoy.

With his hand nestled in mine, August drove away from the curb. He resurrected the hope that had withered from so many years of disappointment. I was done allowing life to happen to me and was ready to shape the life I wanted and August had an important place in this new chapter.

Life wasn't perfect but I finally realized that it could still be wonderful, in spite of the bumps in the road, wrong turns, and missed exits. The best narrator for my life was me, so no more holding the years at bay, waiting for the other shoe to drop, tempering my expectations so that I wasn't let down. I had a new story to tell and I planned to bring every page to life.

epilogue

AUGUST

AFTER MONTHS OF SWEAT EQUITY, Gus and Sly's Auto Shop was opened for business, and to celebrate we hosted a huge grand opening for friends, family, and the neighborhood residents. There were burgers and hot dogs on the grill and a bounce house in the parking lot for the kids. I'd even convinced Sly to rent an ice cream truck that was offering up sweet treats.

We couldn't have pulled this party off without Seraphina's help. I didn't know the first thing about organizing a function like this. But Seraphina was a lifesaver; she created flyers and emailed invites. She found a face painter to draw on the kids' faces. With the community out in full force to support us, I was even more certain that this shop was the right move.

Searching the crowd, I found Seraphina surrounded by my sisters. Making my way over to her, I thought it best to come to her rescue.

"Could we save the interrogation for another time?" I asked, wrapping my arm around Seraphina's shoulder.

Janette gave me a face. "I'm sorry Auggie but when were you gonna tell us you had a girlfriend?"

"More importantly, how did you bag a woman like Seraphina?" Deidre chimed in.

"That's a good question. I guess I just got it like that," I said.

"I used to change this boy's diapers, by the way." Deidra commented to Seraphina.

My middle sister Kim decided to get in on the fun. "Ooo, tell her about the time August peed his pants at Disneyland."

"You peed your pants at Disneyland?"

"I was six and I told you guys I really had to go." I shook my fist for emphasis.

"Excuses, excuses." Kim teased.

"Seraphina told us you two moved in together."

My sisters were nosy and I was far too busy to answer their probing questions. "You know what, they just put out more of those meatballs you like so much." I let my sisters know, hoping the possibility of food would distract them so that I could safely extract Seraphina from their clutches. "There's also fresh potato salad on the table."

"OK but who made it? Cause you know I don't eat just anybody's potato salad," Deidra asked.

I hitched my shoulders. "I don't know."

"Let's go check it out. If it's nasty you're gonna hear about it." Janette mushed me in the side of my head as she and my sisters headed to the corner of the parking lot where the grill and buffet table were set up.

Rubbing Seraphina's shoulders, I said, "I'm sorry. I hoped to ease you into meeting the Gardner sisters. They can be a lot. And they're super overprotective of me. It's like having five extra moms."

"No, I think they're great. Loud and funny, they remind me of my Aunties."

"So they haven't scared you off with stories of me peeing my pants and having an imaginary friend until I was ten?"

"You had an imaginary friend?"

"I wasn't good at making friends so I created one."

"What was his name?"

"She was a girl. Her name was Jett with two T's and she was a tomboy."

Seraphina broke into uncontrollable laughter.

"It's not that funny. No one wanted to play with me growing up. It was a mostly white neighborhood and I stuck out like a sore thumb."

"No ... yeah but it is." Seraphina stopped mid chuckle, her eyes growing wide as she looked past me. "Your mother's here with my grandfather."

I turned on my heels to find my mother and Mr. Jacobs getting out of a cab. Of course, I'd invited my mother and Seraphina offered to pick her up from the home but she seemed reluctant to make the trip. Grabbing hold of Seraphina's hand, we headed over to the sidewalk where my mother stood looking up at the sign on the front of the shop.

"Mom, what are you doing here?"

"Well, you didn't think we were gonna miss your special day." She gave my cheek a quick touch.

At Summercrest some residence could leave the facility at will to run errands or have lunch with a friend. The facility was half nursing home, half assisted living. In my mother's case she still went shopping and made visits to the library all without assistance. Mr. Jacobs on the other hand could only leave Summercrest with permission and never unattended because of his Alzheimer's. How my mother managed to get that man a day pass was beyond me, but with six children she was always resourceful.

"If I knew you were gonna come, I would have picked you up," I said.

"If she had done that we wouldn't have been able to see the surprised look on your face," Mr. Jacobs said, looking around the space with people mingling, and children laughing while loud music blasted from the speakers. I wondered how long it had been since he'd been outside of the Summercrest grounds. From the stunned look on Seraphina's face, I took it that it had indeed been a while.

"This is so special, baby. Show me the shop." My mother said.

Hooking my hand with hers I showed her what I'd been working so hard on all these months. Her being here lifted the weight that was heavy on my shoulders. All I wanted was to see my mother the way she'd always been, vibrant and full of life. Summercrest seemed to dim that glow, but today in the parking lot of my shop it was clear that she was still very much alive and kicking.

Seraphina

"DAD, DO YOU REMEMBER POPS?" I asked, pretending to introduce my father to his father. It had been so long since the two had been in the same space, an introduction was probably needed.

"Hello Herman how have you been?" Pops asked.

"I've been well, Dad. Nice to see you out and about."

"Yep, I escaped. Climbed out the window and crawled through some rose bushes."

I laughed nervously. "That's a joke. Right? You're joking?" With Pops it was hard to tell, he was known for causing trouble.

"You two should catch up." Excusing myself, I went in search of August. I found him in the shop staring into the parking lot. "You good?"

"Yeah, just a little bit shocked that I was able to pull this off."

"Of course you did. I've never seen someone work as hard as you to open this place on time," I said, slipping my hand in his.

"And then my mother's here with your grandfather. That's weird as fuck." August looked at me. "You know in an alternate timeline we could have been related."

I pushed at him playfully. But I definitely spent time drafting a timeline, to include affair dates and birthdates just to be certain August wasn't my granduncle or something. Staring into the parking lot, I located my father and Pops sharing a laugh near the bounce house. I knew it would be a long road to get them back on good terms but every journey had to start somewhere. Who knows maybe one of these days Dad would make the trip to Summercrest with August and I.

Turning to August I tilted his chin toward me. "I'm proud of you."

"I'm proud of *us*."

"Us?"

"Yeah, for finding each other and making it work."

"Well to be fair I'm pretty easy to love."

A smile pulled at the corners of his mouth. Walking to the vending machine, August fished change out of his pocket dropping several coins into the soda machine. The gears whirled before coming to a halt. "Damnit."

"What?"

"This machine won't drop my soda."

Pretending to roll up my sleeves I said, "These machines are sneaky bastards." With a swing of my hips, I hit the machine and the bottle dropped into the receptacle.

"How do you do that?" He looked at me in awe.

"It's really all in the hips." I winked, before planting a juicy kiss on his lips.

thank you. let's connect.

Thank you so much for reading Holding Back The Years. If you liked the book, please help a sister out and leave a review or tell a friend. Your feedback is important to me and will help other readers decide whether to read my book too.

Feel free to connect with me virtually. I would love to engage with you.

instagram.com/authorkashathompson

tiktok.com/@authorkashathompson

twitter.com/thomkat29

also by kasha thompson

Working Through It

Figure of Speech

www.ingramcontent.com/pod-product-compliance
Lightning Source LLC
Chambersburg PA
CBHW031539310726
48971CB00008B/2544